The Briefcase

The Briefcase

By
Hiromi Kawakami

Translated by Allison Markin Powell

COUNTERPOINT | BERKELEY, CALIFORNIA

Excerpts from Seihaku Irako's poetry appear with permission from the
translators, William Elliott and Katsumasa Nishihara. The excerpts on pages 8
and 9 from "Wandering" are reprinted from *The Singing Heart: An Anthology of
Japanese Poems, 1900–1960* © 2006.

Library of Congress Cataloging-in-Publication Data

Kawakami, Hiromi, 1958-
[Sensei no kaban. English]
The briefcase / Hiromi Kawakami ; translated by Allison Markin Powell.
p. cm.

ISBN 978-1-58243-599-2 (pbk.)
1. Women-Fiction. 2. Men-Fiction. 3. Japan-Fiction. I. Powell, Allison Markin. II.
Title.

PL855.A859S4613 2012
895.6'36-dc23

2011041521

Cover design by Gopa & Ted2
Interior design by Domini Dragoone
Printed in the United States of America

COUNTERPOINT
1919 Fifth Street
Berkeley, CA 94710
www.counterpointpress.com
Distributed by Publishers Group West

10 9 8 7 6 5 4 3 2 1

Contents

The Moon and the Batteries

HIS FULL NAME was Mr. Harutsuna Matsumoto, but I called him "Sensei." Not "Mr." or "Sir," just "Sensei."

He was my Japanese teacher in high school. He wasn't my homeroom teacher, and Japanese class didn't interest me much, so I didn't really remember him. Since graduation, I hadn't seen him for quite a while.

Several years ago, we sat beside each other at a crowded bar near the train station, and after that, our paths would cross every now and then. That night, he was sitting at the counter, his back so straight it was almost concave.

Taking my seat at the counter, I ordered "Tuna with fermented soybeans, fried lotus root, and salted shallots," while the old man next to me requested "Salted shallots, lotus root fries, and tuna with fermented soybeans" almost simultaneously. When I glanced over, I saw he was staring right back at me. I thought to myself, *Why do I know his face . . . ?* Sensei spoke.

"Excuse me, are you Tsukiko Omachi?"

Stunned, I nodded in response.

"I've spotted you here sometimes," Sensei said.

"Is that right?" I answered vaguely, still looking at him. His white hair was carefully smoothed back, and he was wearing a starched white shirt with a gray vest. On the counter in front of him, there was a bottle of saké, a plate with a strip of dried whale meat, and a bowl that had a bit of *mozuku* seaweed left in it. I wondered who this old man was who shared the same taste as me, and an image of him standing at a teacher's podium floated through my mind.

Sensei had always held an eraser in his hand when writing on the blackboard. He would write something in chalk, like the first line of *The Pillow Book* by Sei Shonagon: IN SPRING IT IS THE DAWN THAT IS MOST BEAUTIFUL. And then, not five minutes later, he would erase it. Even when he turned to lecture to his students, he would still hold on to the eraser, as if it was attached to his sinewy left hand.

"It's unusual to see a woman alone in a place like this," Sensei said as he delicately poured vinegared miso over the last morsel of dried whale and brought it to his lips with his chopsticks.

"Yes," I replied, pouring beer into my glass. I had identified him as one of my high school teachers, but I still couldn't recall his name. As I drained my glass, part of me marveled that he could remember the name of a particular student, and part of me was puzzled.

"Didn't you wear your hair in braids during high school?"

"Yes."

"I recognized you as soon as I saw you here."

"Oh."

"Did you recently turn thirty-eight this year?"

"I'm still only thirty-seven."

"I'm sorry, I beg your pardon."

"Not at all."

"I looked you up in the register and the yearbook, just to be sure."

"I see."

"You look just the same, you know."

"You look just as well, Sensei." I called him "Sensei" to hide the fact that I didn't know his name. He has been "Sensei" ever since.

That evening, we drank five bottles of saké between us. Sensei paid the bill. The next time we saw each other at the bar and drank together, I treated. The third time, and every time thereafter, we got separate checks and paid for ourselves. That's how it went. We both seemed to be the type of person who liked to stop in every so often at the local bar. Our food preferences weren't the only things we shared; we had a similar rhythm, or temperament. Despite the more than thirty-year difference in our ages, I felt much more familiar with him than with friends my own age.

I WENT TO Sensei's house several times. Every so often we would leave our usual bar to drink at a second place, and then we would go our separate ways home. But the few times we got as far as a third or fourth bar, we inevitably ended up having the final drink at Sensei's house.

"I live nearby, why don't you come over?" Sensei said the first time he invited me to his home, and I felt a twinge of reticence. I had heard that his wife had passed away. The idea of spending time at a widower's home was slightly off-putting, but once I've started drinking, not much can stop me, so I went along.

It was more cluttered than I had imagined. I had thought his place would be immaculate, but there were things piled up in every dark corner. Just off the hall, a carpeted room with an old sofa was absolutely silent and gave no hint of the books and writing paper and newspapers strewn about the adjacent tatami room.

Sensei pulled out the low dining table and took a large bottle of saké from among the things in a corner of the room. He filled two different-sized teacups to the brim.

"Please have a drink," Sensei said before he headed off to the kitchen. The tatami room gave on to a garden. Only one of the rain shutters was open. Through the glass door I could see the vague shape of tree branches. Since they were not in flower, I couldn't tell what kind of trees they were. I've never known much about plants.

"What kind of trees are those in the garden?" I asked Sensei as he carried in a tray with flakes of salmon and *kaki no tane* rice crackers.

"They're all cherry trees," he answered.

"All cherry trees?"

"Yes, all of them. My wife loved them."

"They must be beautiful in the spring."

"They are crawling with insects. In the fall there are dead leaves all over the place, and in winter the bare branches are bleak and dreary," Sensei said without any particular distaste.

"The moon is out tonight." A hazy half-moon hung high in the sky.

Sensei took one of the rice crackers and tilted his teacup as he refilled it with saké. "My wife was the kind of person who didn't think things through."

"I see."

"She just loved the things she loved, and hated the things she hated."

"Oh."

"These *kaki no tane* are from Niigata. They're good and spicy."

The piquant burn of the crackers really did go quite well with saké. I sat there silently for a while, eating them with my fingers. Something fluttered in a treetop outside. It must have been a bird. I heard a faint chirping and the sound of the leaves on the branches rustling for a moment, and then it was quiet again.

"Are there birds' nests?" I asked, but there was no answer. I turned around, and Sensei was gazing at a newspaper. Not today's paper, but one that he had randomly taken from the ones strewn about. He was intently reading a page from the foreign news service that had a photograph of a woman in a bathing suit. He seemed to have forgotten that I was there.

"Sensei," I called, but still there was no response. He was completely absorbed.

"Sensei," I said again in a loud voice. Sensei looked up.

"Would you like to read the newspaper, Tsukiko?" he asked me abruptly. Without waiting for me to reply, Sensei laid the open paper on the tatami, slid open the fusuma, and went into the next room. He came back carrying several things he had taken from an old bureau. They were small pieces of pottery. Sensei made a few trips back and forth between this and the next room.

"Yes, here they are." Sensei crinkled the corners of his eyes, carefully lining up the ceramics on the tatami. They each had a handle, a lid, and a spout. "Look at them!"

"I see." But what *were* they? I stared at them, thinking to myself that I had seen something like these before. They were all roughly made. Were they teapots? But they were so small.

"These are railway teapots," Sensei said.

"Railway teapots?"

"These are from trips I took. I bought box lunches at the station or on the train that came with these teapots. Now the teapots are plastic, but they used to sell them with ceramic railway teapots like these."

There were more than a dozen railway teapots lined up. Some were amber-colored, some were other pale shades. They were all different shapes. This one had a large spout, that one a big handle, this pot had a tiny lid, that pot was fat and round.

"Do you collect them?" I asked, and Sensei shook his head.

"They just came with the box lunches I bought while I was on whatever trip I was taking.

"This one is from the year I started university, when I was traveling around Shinshu. Here is one from when I went to Nara with a colleague during summer vacation—I got off the train at one point to get lunch in the station for both of us, and the train departed just as I was about to get back on! That one was bought in Odawara on my honeymoon—my wife carried it for the whole trip, wrapped in newspaper and stuffed among the clothes in her suitcase, so that it wouldn't break," Sensei explained, pointing to each of the railway teapots lined up in a row. I could only nod and murmur a response to each story.

"I hear there are people who collect these kinds of things."

"Is that why you still have them?"

"Of course not! I would never engage in such crazy whims!"

Crinkling his eyes again, Sensei went on to say, "I was simply showing you some things that I've had for a very long time.

"I just can't seem to throw anything away," Sensei said, going again to the room next door and this time bringing back several small plastic bags.

"See here . . . ," he said as he untied the knot at the opening of one of the plastic bags. He took out what was inside, which were all old batteries. Each of them had written on the side things like ELECTRIC SHAVER, WALL CLOCK, RADIO, or FLASHLIGHT in black magic marker. He took a size-C battery in his hand.

"This battery is from the year of the Ise Bay typhoon. The typhoon hit Tokyo much harder than expected, and that summer I used up the batteries in my flashlight."

He went on, explaining, "The first cassette recorder I ever bought required eight C batteries, which it ate right through. I would listen to Beethoven's symphonies over and over again, and I used up the batteries in just a few days! Of course, I couldn't keep all eight batteries, so I decided to just save one, which I picked out from the bunch with my eyes closed.

"I feel pity for these batteries that worked so hard for my benefit, and I can't throw them away. It seems a shame to get rid of them the moment they die, after these batteries have illuminated my lights, signaled my sounds, and run my motors.

"Don't you think so, Tsukiko?" Sensei asked, peering at me.

I wondered how to answer, as I murmured acknowledgment for the umpteenth time that evening. I touched one of the dozens of batteries of all sizes with the tip of my finger. It was rusty and damp. This one had CASIO CALCULATOR written on it.

"The moon has really sunk low," Sensei said, craning his neck. The moon had emerged from the haze and was glowing clearly.

"I bet the tea from the railway teapots tasted good," I said softly.

"Shall we have some tea now?" Sensei said, suddenly reaching out his hand. Rummaging around where the large saké bottle had been, he pulled out a tea canister. Nonchalantly, he put some tea leaves into the amber railway teapot, then took the lid off of an old thermos that was beside the table and poured in some hot water.

"A student gave me this thermos. It's an old American model, but the boiled water I put in there yesterday is still hot. That's pretty impressive."

Sensei poured tea into the cups out of which we had been drinking saké and then rubbed the thermos as if it were a precious item. There must have been a little saké left in my cup, because the tea had an odd taste. All of a sudden I felt the effects of the alcohol, and I became thoroughly pleased by what I saw around me.

"Sensei, may I take a look around?" Without waiting for Sensei to answer, I delved into the universe of things strewn about the tatami room. There was scrap paper. An old Zippo lighter. A rusted-over pocket mirror. There were three large black leather bags, each with well-worn creases. They were all exactly the same. There were floral shears. A stationery desk. And a black plastic thing shaped like a box. It had calibrations on it and a needle.

"What is this?" I asked, picking up the black calibrated box.

"Let me see . . . Oh, that. It's a tester."

"A tester?" I repeated, as Sensei gently took the black box from my hand and rummaged among some things. Once he located a black and a red cord, he attached each of them to the tester. Both cords had terminals on the ends.

"Go like this," Sensei said, putting the red cord's terminal on one end and the black cord's terminal on the other end of the battery that said ELECTRIC SHAVER.

"See, Tsukiko, look at that!" Since both of his hands were full, Sensei gestured with his chin at the battery tester's calibrations. The needle was just barely vibrating. He moved the terminals away from the battery and the needle went still, and when he touched them again, it quivered.

"There's still a charge left, isn't there?" Sensei said softly. "It's not enough power to run a motor, but there's still a bit of life in it."

Sensei measured each of the many batteries with the tester. Most of them didn't register on the meter when he touched the terminals, but every so often the needle would move. Each time it did, he would utter a little "Oh!"

"The slightest sign of life," I said, and Sensei gave a vague nod.

"But they will all die out eventually," he said languidly, in a far-away voice.

"They'll live out their time inside the dresser."

"I suppose you're right."

We both sat there for a moment, staring silently at the moon, until Sensei finally said cheerfully, "Shall we have another drink?" He poured saké into our cups.

"Oops, there was still some tea left."

"Saké cut with tea, right?"

"But saké doesn't need to be cut with anything."

"It's quite all right, Sensei."

As I murmured "Quite all right, quite all right," I drank the saké in one gulp. Sensei was sipping his. The moon shone brightly on.

Suddenly, in a clear, resonant voice, Sensei recited,

Light filters white across the river
through the willows.
From Ono on the other bank.

"What is that, some kind of sutra?" I asked.

Sensei was indignant. "Tsukiko, you never paid attention in Japanese class, did you?" he said.

"You didn't teach us that," I replied.

"That was Seihaku Irako, you see," Sensei answered in a lecturing tone.

"I've never heard of Seihaku Irako," I said as I took it upon myself to refill my own teacup with saké.

"It's unusual for a woman to pour her own saké," Sensei chided me.

"Oh, Sensei, you're just old!" I retorted.

"Yes, I'm old, and hairy now too!" he mumbled as he too filled his own teacup to the brim.

Then he continued with the poem:

> *From Ono on the other bank*
> *a flute makes its faint way through the mist,*
> *touching the traveler's heart.*

His eyes were closed, as if he too were listening attentively to his recitation. I gazed vacantly at the different batteries. They were silent and still in the pale light. The moon was once again enveloped in haze.

Chicks

SENSEI INVITED ME to go along with him on a market day walk.

"Market days are the eighth, the eighteenth, and the twenty-eighth. This month, the twenty-eighth is a Sunday, so I thought that would suit your schedule," Sensei said, taking his datebook out of the black briefcase he always carried with him.

"The twenty-eighth?" I repeated, slowly leafing through my own datebook, despite the fact that there was nothing at all in my schedule. "Yes, that day is fine," I said with an air of importance. With a big round fountain pen, Sensei wrote on the twenty-eighth in his datebook, MARKET DAY, TSUKIKO, NOON, MINAMI-MACHI BUS STOP. He had excellent penmanship.

"Let's meet at noon," Sensei said as he put the datebook back in his briefcase. It would be unusual to see Sensei in the light of day. Sipping saké side by side in the dimly lit bar while we used our chopsticks to carve away at either chilled or warm tofu, depending on the season—that was how we usually saw each other. We never made plans, but always happened to meet by chance. Weeks went by when our paths didn't cross, and there were stretches when we'd see each other every night.

"What kind of market did you say it is?" I asked while pouring saké into my cup.

"There's only one kind of market, of course. You know, where they sell any kind of household item."

I found it strange to imagine shopping for domestic things with Sensei, but I thought we would be able to get through the day. I too wrote NOON, MINAMI-MACHI BUS STOP in my datebook.

Sensei slowly drained his cup and refilled it himself. He tipped the saké bottle just slightly, which made a gurgling sound as he poured. But he didn't aim the saké bottle right over his cup. Instead, he raised the bottle high over the cup, which sat on the bar, before tipping it. The saké fell in a thin stream, as if being drawn into the cup. He never spilled a drop. It was quite a skill. Once, I tried to imitate Sensei, lifting the saké bottle high and trying to pour, but I spilled almost all of it. It was such a waste. Since then, I grasp my cup firmly with my left hand and pour with the bottle in my right hand, just barely hovering over the cup. I've resigned myself to such gracelessness.

In fact, a former colleague once said to me, "Tsukiko, the way you pour really lacks allure." The word "allure" seemed old-fashioned to me, but then again, the fact that it's always the woman who is expected to pour, and to have "allure" when doing so, seemed antiquated too. I stared at my colleague with surprise. He must have gotten the wrong idea, though, because after we left the bar, he tried to pull me into a dark corner to kiss me. "Cut it out!" I said as I caught his looming face with both my hands and pushed him away.

"There's nothing to be afraid of," he whispered, peeling my hands away and coming in for another try. Everything about him was old-fashioned. It was all I could do to keep from bursting into laughter.

With a deadly serious expression and in an earnest tone, I said, "But today is such an unlucky day."

"Unlucky?"

"Yes, today is a *tomobiki* day. But tomorrow is a red-letter day, a *kanoe-tora*!"

"Huh?"

I took that opportunity to quickly run off toward the subway entrance, leaving my colleague standing agape in the dark street. Even after I was down the stairs, I kept running. After making sure that he wasn't following me, I ducked into the ladies' room. I went to the bathroom and thoroughly washed my hands. As I looked at my reflection in the mirror, with my hair slightly out of place, I started to giggle.

Sensei did not like anyone to pour his drinks for him. Whether it was beer or saké, he meticulously poured for himself. One time, I filled Sensei's first glass of beer for him. The moment I tipped the beer bottle toward his glass, I felt him flinch slightly—actually, more than slightly. But he didn't say a word. When the glass was full, Sensei calmly raised it to his lips, offering a terse "Cheers," and drank it down in one swallow. He downed the whole glassful, but he choked a little. I could tell that he had gulped it down in haste. No doubt he had wanted to finish it off as quickly as possible.

When I picked up the bottle of beer to refill his glass, Sensei sat up straight and said to me, "Thank you, that's very kind. But I enjoy pouring for myself."

I have not poured for him since. But every now and then, he still pours for me.

SENSEI ARRIVED AT the bus stop just after I did. I had gotten there fifteen minutes early, and he got there ten minutes early. It was a beautiful Sunday.

"These elms are so verdant, aren't they?" Sensei said, looking up at the trees beside the bus stop. He was right—dense with leaves, the branches of the elms waved in the breeze. Although the wind was light, high in the sky, the tops of the elms swayed even more grandly.

It was a hot summer day, but the low humidity kept it cool in the shade. We took the bus to Teramachi and then walked a little. Sensei was wearing a panama hat and a Hawaiian shirt in muted colors.

"That shirt looks nice on you," I said.

"Oh, no, it doesn't," Sensei replied tersely, quickening his pace. We walked briskly along beside each other in silence, but then Sensei slowed down to ask, "Are you hungry?"

"Well, actually, I'm a little out of breath," I replied.

Sensei smiled and said, "Well, if you hadn't said such a strange thing."

"I didn't say anything strange. Sensei, you're very well dressed."

Without replying, Sensei went into the boxed-lunch shop in front of us.

"One kimchi pork special," Sensei said to the girl at the counter. He prompted me with his eyes, "And for you?" There were too many things to choose from on the menu—it was bewildering. *Bibimbap* with egg appealed to me at first, but I decided I didn't want a fried egg, which was the only option. After a moment's hesitation, I became paralyzed by the sheer number of choices.

"I'll have the kimchi pork too." Lost in uncertainty, in the end I chose the same thing Sensei had ordered. He and I sat side by side on a bench in a corner of the shop while we waited for our lunches to be prepared.

"Sensei, you seem familiar with the menu here," I said.

He nodded. "I live alone, you know. Do you cook, Tsukiko?"

"I cook when I'm seeing someone," I answered.

Sensei nodded again seriously. "That makes sense. I think it would be good for me to see one or two people."

"Two might be difficult."

"Two would be the limit, I suppose."

During this absurd chat, our lunches had been prepared. The girl put the two boxes, which were different sizes, into a plastic bag with handles. "Why are the boxes different sizes if we ordered the same thing?" I whispered to Sensei.

"But you ordered the regular, not the special, didn't you?" Sensei replied in a low voice. When we went back outside, the wind had picked up a bit. Sensei carried the plastic bag with the boxed lunches in his right hand, and in his left hand he held his panama hat.

STALLS STARTED TO appear here and there on the street. There were stalls that only sold *tabi* boots. Stalls that sold collapsible umbrellas. Stalls for secondhand clothing. Stalls that sold used books mixed with new books. Soon, both sides of the street became tightly packed with stalls.

"You know, forty years ago, all of this was completely destroyed by heavy flooding from a typhoon."

"Forty years ago?"

"Many people died too."

Sensei went on explaining: "The market has been here for a long time. The year after the flood, there were many fewer stalls, but the following year, a full-scale market picked up again on each of the three monthly market days. The market flourished, and now almost all the stalls that used to run from the Teramachi bus stop all the way to the Kawasuji-nishi stop have come back, even on days other than those ending in eight.

"Come on over here," Sensei said, stepping into a small park set away from the street. The park was deserted. Out on the street it teemed with people, but one step inside the park, here was a silent refuge. Sensei bought two cans of *genmaicha* tea from a machine at the entrance to the park.

We sat next to each other on a bench and took the lids off our lunches. The air immediately filled with the aroma of kimchi.

"Sensei, yours is the special, right?"

"That's what they call it."

"How is it different from the regular?"

We both bent our heads to examine the two boxed lunches.

"There doesn't seem to be much difference at all," Sensei said amiably.

I drank the *genmaicha* slowly. Although there was a breeze, the hot summer day had me craving a drink. The cool tea quenched my thirst as I sipped it.

"The way you're eating that looks delicious," Sensei said with a hint of envy as he watched me drizzle the leftover kimchi sauce over my rice. He had already finished eating.

"Excuse my poor manners."

"It may well be bad manners, but it still looks delicious," Sensei said, as he put the lid back on his empty boxed lunch and replaced the rubber band around it. The park was planted with alternating elm and cherry trees. The park must have been there a long time, because the trees had grown sturdy and tall.

After we passed a corner stall selling odds and ends, more and more of the stalls had grocery items for sale. Stalls selling only beans. Stalls with all different kinds of shellfish. There was a stall that had crates full of little shrimp or crabs. There was a banana stall. Sensei stopped to look at each one. He stood with perfect posture, peering at them from a slight distance.

"Tsukiko, that fish looks fresh."

"There are flies swarming on it."

"That's what flies do."

"Sensei, what about that chicken over there?"

"It's a whole chicken, though. It's too much trouble to pluck the feathers."

We browsed past the stalls, chatting at random. The stalls became even more densely packed. They were tight up against each other, and the voices of the vendors hawking their goods also vied with one another.

"Mom . . . These carrots look yummy," a child said to his mother, who was carrying a shopping basket.

"I thought you hated carrots," the mother said with surprise.

"But these carrots look especially good," the child said brightly.

The proprietor of the stall raised his voice: "What a smart boy! That's right, my vegetables are the best!"

"Those carrots do look good, don't they?" Sensei said as he studied them earnestly.

"They look like any other carrots to me."

"Hmm."

Sensei's panama hat was slightly askew. We walked, carried along by the throngs of people. From time to time, I would lose sight of Sensei amid the crowd. But at least I could rely on always being able to spot the top of his panama hat, so he was easy to find. For his part, Sensei seemed unconcerned about me. Much in the way a dog stops to sniff at every telephone pole, Sensei would simply stop and stare whenever a stall caught his interest.

The mother and child we had seen earlier were now in front of a mushroom stall. Sensei stood right behind them.

"Mom, these *kinugasa* mushrooms look yummy."

"I thought you hated *kinugasa* mushrooms."

"But these *kinugasa* mushrooms look especially good." They went through exactly the same exchange.

"They must be decoy plants," Sensei said gleefully.

"That's pretty ingenious, to use a mother-and-child setup."

"But '*kinugasa* mushrooms,' that was over-the-top."

"Yes."

"They should have used *maitake* mushrooms instead."

The grocery stalls thinned and gave way to stalls selling larger items. Household appliances. Computers. Telephones. There were mini refrigerators lined up in different colors. An LP was playing on an old record player. I could hear the low timbre of a violin. The music had an old-fashioned, simple charm. Sensei stood, listening intently, until the end of the piece.

IT WAS STILL only mid-afternoon, yet there were already almost imperceptible signs of the approaching evening. The hottest part of the day had just passed.

"Are you thirsty?" Sensei asked.

"Yes, but if we're going to be drinking beer this evening, I don't want anything else to drink before then," I replied.

Sensei nodded in satisfaction. "Good answer."

"Was that a test?"

"Tsukiko, you are an excellent student when it comes to drinking. In Japanese class, on the other hand, your grades were awful . . ."

There was a stall that had cats for sale. There were newborn kittens and great big fat cats. A child was pleading with his mother for a cat. It was the mother and child from earlier.

"We don't have anywhere to keep a cat," the mother said.

"That's okay, it can be an outdoor cat," the child replied softly.

"But do you really think a cat we buy here can survive outside?"

"It'll be all right, somehow." The owner of the cat stall listened in silence to their conversation. Finally, the child pointed at a small, striped tabby. The owner wrapped the tabby in a soft cloth and the mother took it and gently placed it in her shopping basket. The faint sound of the tabby's mewling could be heard from inside the basket.

"Tsukiko," Sensei said suddenly.

"Yes?"

"I'm going to buy something too."

Sensei approached not the cat stall, but a stall selling chicks.

"Male and female, one chick each," Sensei said decisively.

The proprietor of the stall picked one each from the two separate groups of chicks on either side, and placed each chick into its own little box. "Here you are," he said as he handed them to Sensei, who took the boxes cautiously. Holding them in his left hand, Sensei pulled his wallet from his pocket with his right hand and gave it to me.

"Would you mind paying him for me?"

"Why don't I hold the boxes?"

"Ah, yes."

Sensei's panama hat was even more askew now. Wiping the sweat from his brow with a handkerchief, he took out the money to pay. He put his wallet back in his breast pocket and, after a moment's hesitation, he took off his panama hat.

Sensei turned his hat upside down. Then he took the chicks' boxes one at a time from my hands and put them inside the upside down hat. Once the boxes were settled, Sensei began walking with the hat carried protectively under his arm.

We got on the bus at the Kawasuji-nishi stop. There were fewer people on the bus ride home than on the way there. The market surged again with people who were probably doing their evening shopping.

"I've heard that it's difficult to tell the difference between a male and a female chick," I said, and Sensei made a sort of harrumphing sound.

"Well, I know that much."

"Oh."

"It doesn't matter to me whether these chicks are male or female."

"I see."

"I thought one chick would be lonely on its own."

"Really?"

"Really."

Was that so? I wondered as I got off the bus and followed Sensei into our usual bar. "Two bottles of beer," Sensei ordered right away. "And edamame." The beer and our glasses came right out.

"Sensei, shall I pour?" I asked, but he shook his head.

"No. I'll pour for you, Tsukiko. And I'll pour for myself too." As usual, he wouldn't let me pour for him.

"Do you hate it when someone else pours?"

"I don't mind if they can do it well, but you aren't very good at it."

"Is that right?"

"Would you like me to teach you?"

"That's not necessary."

"You're a stubborn one."

"As are you."

There was a stiff head of foam on the beer that Sensei poured for me. "Where will you keep the chicks?" I asked. "Inside the house, for now," Sensei replied. I could barely hear the sound of the chicks moving inside the box, inside the hat. "Do you like having pets?" I asked. Sensei shook his head.

"I don't think it's my forte."

"Will you be able to handle them?"

"Chicks aren't very cute, are they?"

"Is it better if they aren't cute?"

"That way I won't become obsessive."

There was a rustling sound as the chicks moved again. Sensei's glass was empty, so I replenished it. He did not refuse. "A little more foam. That's right." He talked me through the technique as he serenely accepted the beer I poured for him.

"Soon you'll have to let those chicks out somewhere in the open," I said. That night we drank only beer. We had edamame, grilled eggplant, and octopus marinated in wasabi. After we finished eating, we split the check right down the middle.

When we came out of the bar, it was almost dark. I wondered if the mother and child from the market had finished their dinner already. I wondered if the cat was still mewling. There was only a hint of a glow lingering in the western sky.

Twenty-two Stars

SENSEI AND I aren't speaking.

It's not that I haven't seen him. I often run into him at our usual bar, but we don't speak. We glance at each other out of the corner of one eye, and then we simply pretend we are strangers. I pretend, and Sensei pretends as well.

It has been going on since about the time when the bar started serving "Stew of the day" as a special, so it must be almost a month by now. Even when we sit next to each other at the counter, we don't say a word.

IT ALL STARTED with the radio.

The broadcast of the baseball game was on. They were leading up to the final game of the pennant race. It was unusual for the radio to be on in the bar, and I was sitting with my elbows resting on the counter, idly listening to the game while drinking warm saké.

Before long, the door opened and Sensei came in. He took the seat next to me and asked the bar owner, "What's in the stew?" There were several dented individual-sized aluminum pots piled up on the cupboard.

"Cod stew today."

"That sounds good."

"So, would you like the stew then?" the bar owner asked, but Sensei shook his head.

"I'll have salted sea urchin."

He certainly is unpredictable, I thought to myself as I listened to their exchange. The first-at-bat team's third batter got an extra base hit, and the sound of cheering and the fife and drum-playing grew louder on the radio.

"Tsukiko, which is your favorite team?"

"None in particular," I replied, filling my cup with warm saké. Everyone in the bar was listening to the radio ardently.

"Obviously, it's the Giants for me," Sensei said, draining his beer in one gulp and switching to saké. He spoke—how can I put it?—with more passion than usual. I wondered about this passion.

"Obviously?"

"Yes, obviously."

The game on the broadcast was the Yomiuri Giants versus the Hanshin Tigers. I don't have a favorite team, but to tell the truth, I hate the Giants. I used to openly proclaim myself "anti-Giants." But one time, someone pointed out that being "anti-Giants" was really just a backward strategy for those who were so stubborn they couldn't bring themselves to say that they liked the Giants. Something about this resonated with me, and, since then, I have refrained from even uttering the dreaded name, "Giants." I avoid baseball broadcasts. Honestly, the issue is so murky in my own mind that I myself am not at all certain whether I love or hate the Giants.

Sensei lingered over his bottle of saké. Whenever the Giants' pitcher struck out a batter, or a Giants player got a hit, he nodded vigorously.

"What's the matter, Tsukiko?" Sensei asked me after a home run at the top of the seventh inning gave the Giants a three-point lead over the Tigers.

"I'm just tapping my foot."

I had been nervously shaking my foot since the Giants had gained their lead.

"The nights are getting cold," I said, apropos of nothing and not even in Sensei's direction, but more toward the ceiling. At that moment, the player for the Giants got another hit. Sensei cried out "Oh!" just as I muttered "Shit!" without meaning to. This run gave them a secure four-run lead, and the bar exploded with excitement. Why were Giants fans so ubiquitous? It really was annoying.

"Tsukiko, do you hate the Giants?" Sensei asked me at the bottom of the ninth, when the Tigers were down to their last out. I nodded, not saying a word. The bar had calmed down. Almost everyone there was listening closely to the broadcast. I had a disquieting feeling. It had been a long time since I had listened to a baseball game on the radio, and my Giants-hating blood was boiling over. I now knew for sure that it was, in fact, straightforward hatred as opposed to some kind of perverse affectation.

"I can't stand them," I said in a low voice.

Sensei's eyes opened wide. "How can you be Japanese and hate the Giants?!" he murmured.

"What kind of prejudice is that?" I asked, just as the Tigers' last batter struck out. Sensei stood up from his chair and raised his glass high. Over the radio, they announced the end of the game, and the bar started bustling again. Suddenly, orders for drinks and food came from every direction, the owner replying to each one with a gruff acknowledgment.

"They won, Tsukiko!" Sensei beamed and moved to fill my cup with saké from his own bottle, which was rather unusual. We had established a practice of never encroaching on each other's food or drink. We ordered on our own. We poured for ourselves. And we paid separately. We had been doing it this way all this time. But here was Sensei coming over to pour me his saké, to break our tacit agreement. And it was all because the Giants had won. It was far too soon for me to have Sensei so capriciously endanger the comfortable distance that existed between us. Those fucking Giants.

"So what?" I said very quietly as I tried to move my cup away from Sensei.

"Nagashima's a great manager, isn't he?" Sensei still managed to deftly pour his saké into my fleeing cup, without spilling a drop. Quite well done.

"Fortunately that's fortunate," I said, turning aside and putting down the cup of saké without drinking it.

"Tsukiko, that's a strange thing to say."

"Unfortunately that's unfortunate."

"The pitcher played well, too." Sensei was laughing.

He's laughing—what a jerk, I cursed to myself. Sensei had a huge grin on his face. And Sensei, who was always so calm and composed, was laughing heartily.

"Can we stop talking about it?" I said, staring at Sensei. But he wouldn't stop grinning. And there was something curious playing at the corners of his mouth. It was like the glimmer of delight in the eyes of a young boy as he squashes little ants.

"No, I will not stop talking about it, most definitely not!"

What was he saying? Sensei knew that I hated the Giants, and here he was, gloating. He was most definitely gloating.

"The Giants, they're all fuckers," I said, spilling the entire cup of saké that Sensei had poured me onto an empty plate.

"'Fuckers'?! Such language from a young lady!" Sensei replied, having regained his perfect composure. He stood up even straighter than usual and drained his cup.

"I am not a young lady."

"Pardon me."

Disquiet filled the air between Sensei and me. Sensei did have a point. After all, the Giants had won. Eventually, without saying a word, we each went back to pouring our own drinks. We didn't order anything to eat, we simply kept on pouring. At the end of the night, we were both quite drunk. Maintaining our silence, we each paid our bill, left the bar, and went our respective ways home. And ever since then, we haven't spoken.

WHEN I THOUGHT about it, Sensei was the only person I spent any time with.

For a while now, there hadn't been anyone besides Sensei with whom I had sat and had a drink, or gone for a walk, or seen anything interesting.

When I tried to think whom I spent time with before I became friendly with Sensei, no one came to mind.

I had been alone. I rode the bus alone, I walked around the city alone, I did my shopping alone, and I drank alone. And even when I was with Sensei now, I didn't feel any different than when I did these things on my own. It seemed, then, that it didn't really matter whether or not I was with Sensei, but the truth was, doing these things with him made me feel proper. "Proper" is perhaps a strange way to put it. It was more like the way I felt about leaving the extra band, the *obi*, that sometimes came on a book jacket intact after I bought it, rather than throwing it away. Sensei would probably be angry if he knew I was comparing him to the band on a dust jacket.

When I saw Sensei at the bar and we pretended not to know each other, it felt as distressing as if the ripped-off band and book were lying strewn about on the ground. But it would have been too wearisome to attempt to restore the level of comfort we had. No doubt Sensei felt the same way. And so we just went on ignoring each other.

I HAD TO go to Kappabashi for work. There was a strong wind that day. I was wearing a light jacket but I was still cold. It wasn't a plaintive autumn wind, but rather a rough wind, calling winter to mind. Kappabashi is filled with wholesale dealers of household goods and tableware. There are pots and kettles, plates and bowls, and all sorts of small kitchenware. After I finished my work errands, I walked around, window-shopping. One store had copper pots that were nested inside each other, smaller and smaller versions of the same pot piled up one on top of the next. The front of another store was decorated with huge earthenware pots. Yet another had spatulas and ladles, arranged by size. There was a cutlery store. Kitchen knives, vegetable knives, sashimi knives—all of them were displayed, without their handles, inside the glass door. There were nail clippers too, and floral shears.

Attracted by the gleaming blades, I went into the store. In one corner was an assortment of graters. There were dozens of graters of different sizes, grouped together by the handles, with a little piece of cardboard that said GRATERS ON SALE attached to each bunch with a rubber band.

"How much is this?" I held up a small grater and asked the sales clerk.

"One thousand yen," she answered. The sales clerk was wearing an apron. "Sales tax included, it's exactly ¥1,000." When she said, "sales tax," it sounded like "tales sax." I paid with a thousand-yen note and she wrapped it up for me.

I already had a grater. Kappabashi was the kind of place where I couldn't resist buying something every time I came. On one trip, I bought a huge iron pot. I had thought it would be useful to have when I cooked for a lot of people, but when did I ever have that many people at my apartment? And even if I did, I hadn't considered that I wouldn't know what to make in a big pot that I wasn't accustomed to cooking with. And so it sat, unused, in the back of the kitchen cupboard.

I had bought the new grater because I wanted to give it to Sensei. I had started to miss Sensei while looking at the brilliant knives.

As I gazed at the blades, so sharp that touching them would draw blood instantly, the desire to see Sensei grew. I had no idea why the gleam of the knives elicited such a feeling, but I missed him intensely. I was seized by the thought of buying a kitchen knife and bringing it to Sensei at home, but a big knife seemed ill-matched for that house. Somehow it didn't suit the dimness and dampness of the atmosphere there. But the fine-toothed grater was just right. And at exactly ¥1,000, it was perfect. If I were to spend ten times that, and Sensei still ignored me, I would be angry. I didn't think he would be so fickle, but then again, he was a Giants fan. There was no way that I could genuinely trust what he might do.

NOT LONG AFTER that, I ran into Sensei at the bar.

As before, Sensei pretended that he didn't know me. And I too couldn't help but respond in turn.

We were at the counter, two seats away from each other. In between us, a man drank alone while he read the newspaper. On the other side of the newspaper, Sensei ordered *yudofu*. I ordered *yudofu* as well.

"It's cold outside, isn't it?" the bartender said, and Sensei nodded. He may have replied softly, "Yes, it is," but I couldn't hear over the rustling of the newspaper.

"It got chilly all of a sudden," I said over the man with the newspaper, and Sensei cast a glance in my direction. *Well, well . . .* , his expression seemed to say. It would have been the perfect opportunity to nod or smile at him, but I could not bring myself to do so. I quickly looked away. On the other side of the man with the newspaper, I could feel Sensei slowly shifting, his back now to me.

The tofu arrived, and I ate at the same pace as Sensei. I drank at the same pace as him, and I got drunk at the same pace. Since both of us were feeling tense, it took longer than usual for the alcohol to take effect. The man with the newspaper made no move to leave. And Sensei and I, we sat drinking on either side of him, each looking the other way and feigning composure.

"The Japan Series is over, huh," the man said to the bartender.

"Soon it'll be winter."

"I don't like the cold, you know."

"But it's a good time for stew."

The man and the bartender chatted agreeably. Sensei turned his head, as if to look at me. I could feel his gaze becoming more and more insistent. Cautiously, I turned to face him.

"Would you like to come sit over here?" Sensei said in a low voice.

"Yes," I replied, my voice also low.

The seat on the other side of the man with the newspaper, next to Sensei, was empty. I told the bartender that I was moving. I picked up my saké bottle and cup and changed seats.

"Thanks," I said, and Sensei murmured something almost inaudibly in response.

And then, both of us still facing forward, we each resumed drinking our own saké, together.

AFTER WE PAID our separate checks, we parted the shop curtain and stepped outside. It wasn't as cold as I expected, and stars were twinkling in the sky. We had finished drinking later than usual.

"Sensei, here," I said, holding out the package, which was now wrinkled from being carried around for a while.

"What is it?" Sensei took the bundle, placing his briefcase on the ground and carefully unwrapping it. The small grater emerged. It glimmered in the pale light that shone through the shop curtain. It gleamed even more brightly than it had in the shop in Kappabashi.

"It's a grater, isn't it?"

"That's right."

"Is it for me?"

"Of course."

It was a brusque exchange. Which was just like our usual conversation. I looked up at the sky and scratched the top of my head. Sensei carefully rewrapped the grater and put it in his briefcase, then straightened and started walking.

I counted stars as I walked. I counted them, looking up at the sky and trailing behind Sensei. When I reached eight, Sensei said suddenly, "*Plum blossoms, fresh shoots, prepared at Mariko's inn, with grated yam soup.*"

"What is that?" I asked.

Sensei shook his head and lamented, "You don't know your Basho either?"

"That was Basho?" I asked again.

"Yes, it's Basho. I taught you his poetry, a long time ago," he said. I had no recollection of learning that haiku. Sensei started walking faster.

"Sensei, you're walking too fast," I said to his back, but he didn't respond. I deliberately repeated the strange words with a hint of irritation: "Grated yam soup prepared at Mariko's inn."

Sensei kept walking for a moment. Then he stopped, and without turning around, he said, "We should make grated yam soup together sometime. Basho's poem is a spring haiku, but the yams are delicious right now. I can use the grater and, Tsukiko, you can grind them with a mortar and pestle, if you don't mind." His voice was the same as always, though he still stood in front of me, without turning to face me.

I continued to count stars, following along behind Sensei. I was up to about fifteen when we got to the place where we went our separate ways.

"Goodbye," I waved.

Sensei waved back and said, "Goodbye."

I watched his back as he left, and then I headed to my own place. By the time I got home, I had counted twenty-two stars, including even the tiny little ones.

Mushroom Hunting, Part 1

WHAT ON EARTH was I doing, wandering around a place like this?

It was Sensei's fault—after all, he was the one who first starting talking about mushrooms.

We had been sitting at the counter in the bar, the air that evening filled with autumn briskness, when Sensei, his posture perfect as always, said cheerfully, "I love mushrooms."

"*Matsutake* mushrooms?" I asked, but he shook his head.

"*Matsutake* are fine, of course, but . . ."

"Yes?"

"Assuming that 'mushrooms' refers to *matsutake* is as simplistic as deciding that 'baseball' means the Giants."

"But don't you love the Giants, Sensei?"

"I do, but I'm perfectly aware that, objectively, baseball is not only about the Giants."

The quarrel that Sensei and I had over the Giants was still quite recent, and both of us were now extremely cautious when it came to baseball.

"There are many varieties of mushrooms."

"I see."

"For instance, you can pick *murasaki shimeji* mushrooms and roast them on the spot. Drizzled with soy sauce—my goodness, so delicious!"

"Yes."

"And *iguchi* mushrooms are quite savory as well."

"I see."

As our conversation went on, the owner of the bar had poked his head out from his side of the counter.

"You know a lot about mushrooms, sir!"

Sensei gave a slight nod. "Oh, not much at all," he said, although his demeanor seemed to suggest that he knew quite a bit.

"I always go mushroom hunting this time of year," the owner said, craning his neck. He gestured toward Sensei and me with his nose, like a mama bird feeding her chicks.

"I see," Sensei replied in the same vague way that I often did.

"Well then, sir, since you like them so much, would you like to come along with me on this year's mushroom hunt?"

Sensei and I exchanged glances. Despite the fact that we came to this bar almost every other night, the owner had never once treated us like regulars or made a point of making friendly conversation. Rather, it was the kind of place where everyone was treated like a new customer. And now, suddenly, the owner had invited us "to come along" with him.

"Where do you do this mushroom hunting?" Sensei asked.

The owner craned his neck even further. "Around Tochigi," he answered. Sensei and I exchanged glances once again. The owner awaited our reply, his neck still outstretched. At the same moment that I wondered aloud, What do you think . . . ? Sensei responded, Let's go. Somehow, just like that, it was decided that we would go mushroom hunting in Tochigi via the owner's car.

• • •

I KNOW ABSOLUTELY nothing about cars. Neither does Sensei. The bar owner's car was white and boxy, unlike the sort of streamlined cars that you often saw these days in the city. This car was squarish and outdated, and somewhat austere, the kind that was common more than ten years ago.

The plan was to meet up outside the bar at six in the morning on Sunday. So I set my alarm for 5:30 AM and, without even washing my face, grabbed the musty old rucksack that I had dug out from the back of my closet the night before as I left my apartment. The sound of the key as I locked the front door echoed unpleasantly in the morning air. I couldn't stop myself from yawning repeatedly as I headed for the bar.

Sensei had already arrived. He stood there perfectly straight, his briefcase in hand, as always. The trunk of the car was open wide, and the bar owner's upper body was thrust inside.

"Is that equipment for hunting mushrooms?" Sensei asked.

"No," the owner replied, without changing position. "I'm bringing this stuff to my cousin's place in Tochigi." His voice reverberated from within the trunk.

The things he was bringing to his cousin's place in Tochigi consisted of several paper bags and one long, rectangular package. Sensei and I both peered over the owner's shoulder. A crow cried from atop a utility pole. *Caw, caw, caw, caw*, it called, sounding just like a crow. Its voice seemed a bit more carefree than when I heard crows during the daytime.

"These are Soka *senbei* and Asakusa *nori*," the owner said, pointing at the paper bags.

"I see," Sensei and I replied in unison.

"And this is saké." He pointed at the long package.

"Yes," Sensei said, his briefcase hanging straight down. I said nothing.

"My cousin, he really likes Sawanoi saké."

"As do I," Sensei said.

"It's great. But my bar serves Tochigi saké."

The owner seemed much more relaxed than when he was at the bar. He looked at least ten years younger. Hop in, he said, opening the rear door and leaning halfway into the driver's seat to start the car. Once the engine caught, he extricated himself from the front seat and went to close the trunk. He made sure that Sensei and I were settled into the backseat and walked a full circle around the car, then stood there smoking a cigarette before getting in to the driver's seat. He yanked on his seatbelt and slowly stepped on the accelerator.

"Thank you so much for inviting us today," Sensei called out formally from the backseat.

The owner swiveled around, beaming at us. "Let's take it easy." He had a nice smile. But he still had his foot on the gas pedal and the car continued to inch forward while he was completely turned around.

"Um, ahead of you," I murmured, but the owner merely craned his neck in my direction. "Huh?" he asked. Still facing us, he made no effort to glance in front of him. All the while the car continued to glide forward.

Sensei cautioned, "You might want to look ahead," while I cried out at the same time, "Up ahead! Up ahead!" A utility pole was close at hand.

"Oh?!" The owner spun back around and turned the steering wheel just in time to avoid the pole. Sensei and I both gave a deep sigh.

"No worries," the owner said as he sped up. What on earth was I doing here in a stranger's car? And this early in the morning!? I still had no idea what mushroom hunting entailed, and I felt as if I were still drinking. The car sped along faster, despite my confusion.

I MUST HAVE dozed off. When I opened my eyes, we were on a mountain road. I had been awake until we had gotten off the expressway onto a smaller highway that I didn't know the name of. The three of us had chatted intermittently, about the fact that Sensei had taught Japanese, that I had been his student, that my grades in Japanese class had been unremarkable, that the bar owner's name was Satoru, that there were lots of *modashi* mushrooms to be found in the mountains where we were heading. I might have liked to know more about these *modashi* mushrooms, or to share just how strict a teacher Sensei had been, but since Satoru kept turning all the way around whenever he spoke to us, Sensei and I made sure not to seem too interested in eliciting small talk.

The car slowly climbed the mountain road. The windows had been open, but Satoru closed his now. Sensei and I followed suit, rolling up the rear windows. The air had grown slightly chilly. I could hear the crystalline sound of birdsong from within the mountains. The road gradually narrowed.

We came to a fork in the road. One way was paved, the other way was gravel. Just as we pulled onto the gravel road, the car came to a stop. Satoru got out and walked further up the gravel road. Sensei and I stayed in the backseat as we watched Satoru.

"Where could he be going?" I pondered, and Sensei tilted his head. I opened the window and cool mountain air rushed in. The birds' voices were close. The sun was now high in the sky. It was past nine o'clock.

"Tsukiko, do you think we'll get back?" Sensei said suddenly.

"What?"

"Somehow I have the feeling that we might not make it back home again."

You're not serious, I replied, and Sensei smiled. He fell silent after that, staring at the rearview mirror. You must be tired, I added, but he shook his head.

"Not at all. Not at all!"

"You know, Sensei, it's not too late to turn back."

"'Turn back'? How do you mean?"

"Well . . ."

"Let's go along with this together. No matter where."

"What?"

Was Sensei having a bit of fun? I stole a glance at his face but his expression was the same as always. Calm and reassured. He was sitting up straight, his briefcase lying next to him on the seat. While I puzzled over this, Satoru came down the hill with another person in tow.

The other man was a perfect double of Satoru. The two of them opened the trunk and hurriedly carried the packages up the hill. Just as I thought they were out of sight, they returned, both of them stopping beside the car to puff on cigarettes.

"G'morning!" Satoru's double said as he got into the passenger seat.

"This is my cousin Toru," Satoru introduced him. Toru looked just like him, in every way. His face, his expression, his build, even the air about him—they were exactly alike.

"So, Toru, I hear that you enjoy Sawanoi saké," Sensei said.

With his seatbelt fastened, Toru twisted himself around to face the back. "That's right, I sure do!" he replied cheerfully.

"But saké from Tochigi is still better," Satoru added, turning around at the same angle as Toru. The car had started up the mountain road. Just as Sensei and I each let out a cry, the front end of the car scraped up against the guardrail.

"Idiot," Toru muttered nonchalantly. Satoru smiled as he turned the steering wheel. Sensei and I let out another sigh. I could hear muffled birdsong from the forest.

"SENSEI, ARE YOU going to hike in those clothes?"

We had driven for another thirty minutes or so after Toru joined us, then Satoru had stopped the car and turned off the engine. Satoru, Toru, and I were all wearing jeans and sneakers. We got out of the car, and the two of them started bending their knees and stretching their legs. I followed their lead. Only Sensei stood still, completely upright. He wore a tweed suit with leather shoes. His suit looked old but well-tailored.

"You'll get dirty," Toru continued.

"It does not matter if I get dirty," Sensei replied, shifting his briefcase from his right hand to his left hand.

"Would you like to leave your briefcase?" Satoru asked.

"That won't be necessary," Sensei replied imperturbably.

Without further ado, we started to climb the wooded path. Satoru and Toru both wore similar rucksacks on their backs. Theirs were climbing daypacks, about one size larger than the one I was carrying. Toru led the way, and Satoru brought up the rear.

"The ascent is surprisingly tough going," Satoru said from behind.

"Uh ... Yes, it is," I said, as Toru said from ahead in the exact same voice, "Easy, just take your time."

Every so often I could hear a sound like *ta-ra-ra-ra-ra, ta-ra-ra-ra-ra*. Sensei kept a steady pace as he climbed along the path. He wasn't particularly out of breath. I, on the other hand, was considerably winded. The *ta-ra-ra-ra-ra, ta-ra-ra-ra-ra* became more insistent.

"Is that a cuckoo?" Sensei asked.

Toru turned around to reply. "No, actually, that's a woodpecker. Sensei, you must know a lot about birds to recognize a cuckoo's call."

He went on, "That's the sound the woodpecker makes when he pecks at a tree trunk, looking for insects to eat."

"He makes quite a racket," Satoru said from behind, laughing.

The path grew steeper and steeper. It was about as narrow as an animal trail. Autumn grasses had grown thick on either side, and they brushed against our faces and hands as we walked along. At the foot of the mountain, the fall foliage had yet to change but up here most of the leaves were tinged red or yellow. The air was cool and pleasant, but I had broken into a sweat, due to the fact that I never exercised. Sensei, however, appeared quite relaxed, carrying his briefcase lightly in one hand.

"Sensei, do you do a lot of mountain climbing?"

"Tsukiko, this is not what one calls mountain climbing."

"I see."

"Look, there's the sound of the woodpecker eating insects again."

I chose not to look, instead keeping my head down as I continued to walk along. Toru called out (or was it Satoru?—I was looking down and couldn't tell from which way the voice came), "Sensei, you're doing well."

Then Satoru called out (or was it Toru?) in encouragement, "Keep it up, Tsukiko, you're much younger than Sensei."

The path seemed like it would go on forever. The *ta-ra-ra-ra-ra* was now interspersed with calls of *chi-chi-chi*, and *ryu-ryu-ryu-ryu-ryu*, and *gu-ru-ru-ru-ru*.

"We're almost there, aren't we?" Toru said.

"I'm sure it's right around here," Satoru replied. Toru suddenly veered off the path. We traipsed into an area where there were no tracks of any sort. Just one step off the path, the air suddenly felt dense and thick.

"They're around here, so keep your eyes on the ground," Toru said as he turned around.

"Be careful not to trample them," Satoru added from behind.

The ground was moist and damp. After walking a little bit, the undergrowth became sparse and instead there were clusters of trees. Here it was a gentle incline, and much easier to walk without the grasses catching at my steps.

"I've found something!" Sensei cried out. Toru and Satoru ambled their way closer to Sensei.

"Well, that's unusual," Toru said as he crouched down.

"Is it a *Cordyceps sinensis*?" Sensei asked.

"The caterpillar is still pretty big."

"It must be some kind of larva."

The three of them exchanged opinions. Under my breath, I muttered, "*Cordyceps sinensis?*"

Sensei took a stick and drew the Japanese name in four large characters on the ground: *Tō CHŪ KA SŌ.* "Winter insect summer plant. Tsukiko, you weren't listening very closely in science class, either, were you?" he scolded.

Nobody ever taught us that in class. I pouted.

Toru burst into laughter. "They don't teach the really important things in school, do they now?" he said. Sensei stood erect as he listened to Toru's guffaws.

Finally, he said quietly, "A person can learn all manner of things, no matter where he finds himself, provided his spirit is determined."

"Your teacher, he's hilarious, you know?" Toru said, having himself another good laugh. Sensei took a plastic bag out of his briefcase and quietly put the *Cordyceps* in it, tying off the top. He put it back into his briefcase.

"All right then, we're going in further. We have to, if we want to find enough to fill our bellies with," Satoru said, stepping between the trees. The rest of us fell out of line, everyone looking at our feet as we moved forward. Sensei's tweed suit blended in among the trees, providing him with a sort of natural camouflage. Even when I thought he was directly in front of me, if I happened to look away, I would quickly lose sight of him. Wondering where he'd gone, I'd look around to find him standing right beside me.

"Sensei, there you are, right here," I'd call out to him, and he'd respond in a strange voice, "I'm not going anywhere," trailing off in a chuckle. Within the forest, Sensei seemed quite different from his usual self. He was like a woodland creature who had lived among the trees since ancient times.

"Sensei," I called out to him again. I felt lonely.

"Tsukiko, didn't I say that I'd stay right by your side?"

Despite what he had said, Sensei—being Sensei—would go on ahead, leaving me behind. Tsukiko, pull yourself together. You always have a bad attitude, he would say as he kept right on moving.

I heard the *ta-ra-ra-ra-ra*, much closer this time. Sensei went off into the trees. Idly, I stood and watched him go. *What am I doing here*, I wondered to myself. I caught a glimpse of Sensei's tweed coat between the trees.

"Inky cap *modashi*!" Satoru shouted from further ahead. "A whole colony of them! Lots more than last year!" Satoru's voice (or was it Toru's?) was full of excitement as it echoed throughout the forest.

Mushroom Hunting, Part 2

I WAS SITTING on a large tree stump and looking up at the sky.

Sensei and Satoru and Toru had all ventured much further into the forest. The *ta-ra-ra-ra-ra* was now off in the distance and in its place I could hear a high-pitched *ru-ru-ru-ru-ru*.

The area where I sat was slick with dampness. It wasn't just that the ground was moist—all around me, it felt like it was bursting—with the leaves on the trees, the undergrowth, the countless microorganisms under the ground, the flat bugs crawling over the surface, the winged insects flitting through the air, the birds perched on branches, even the breath of the larger animals that inhabited the deeper forest.

I could only see a small patch of sky, the part that was left open between the treetops of the forest around me. The branches seemed like a network that in some places almost obscured the sky. Once my eyes had adjusted to the faint light, I realized that the undergrowth was alive with all manner of things. Tiny orange mushrooms. Moss. Something that looked like coarse white veins on the underside of a leaf. What must be some kind of fungus. Dead beetles. Various kinds of ants. Centipedes. Moths on the backs of leaves.

It seemed strange to be surrounded by so many living things. When I was in Tokyo, I couldn't help but feel like I was always alone, or occasionally in the company of Sensei. It seemed like the only living things in Tokyo were big like us. But of course, if I really paid attention, there were plenty of other living things surrounding me in the city as well. It was never just the two of us, Sensei and me. Even when we were at the bar, I tended to only take notice of Sensei. But Satoru was always there, along with the usual crowd of familiar faces. And I never really acknowledged that any of them were alive in any way. I never gave any thought to the fact that they were leading the same kind of complicated life as I was.

Toru came back to where I was sitting.

"Tsukiko, everything okay?" he asked as he showed me the handfuls of mushrooms he had collected.

"Totally fine. Really," I replied.

"Well, I wish you would have come along with us," Toru said.

"Tsukiko can be a tad bit sentimental." The instant I realized this was Sensei's voice, he suddenly and unexpectedly emerged from the shade of the trees just behind me. Whether it was because his suit acted as protective coloring or he was particularly surefooted in the forest, until that moment I had been completely unaware of his presence.

"You were sitting there all alone, lost in your thoughts, weren't you?" Sensei went on. There were fallen leaves stuck here and there on his tweed jacket.

"Do you mean to say she's a girlish romantic?" Toru asked as he roared with laughter.

"Girlish, indeed!" I replied, deadpan.

"Well, then, would the young Miss Tsukiko like to help me prepare the soup?" Toru said, reaching into Satoru's rucksack and taking out an aluminum pot and a portable cooking stove.

"Could you fetch some water?" he asked, and I hurriedly stood up. He told me there was a stream just ahead, so I walked there to find water springing forth among large rocks. Catching some water in my palms, I brought it to my lips. The water was icy cold, yet smooth and mellow. I caught more of it with my palms, bringing it to my lips over and over again.

"HAVE A TASTE," Satoru said to Sensei, who was sitting up straight, Japanese-style, his feet tucked under his legs on a newspaper that had been spread over the ground. Sensei sipped the mushroom soup.

Satoru and Toru had skillfully prepared the mushrooms they had collected. Toru had cleaned the mushrooms of any dirt or mud, and Satoru had torn the large ones into pieces, leaving the smaller ones as they were, before briefly sautéing them in a small frying pan they had also brought along. Then he put the sautéed mushrooms into the pot of already boiling water, stirred in some miso, and let it all simmer for a little while.

"I studied up a bit last night for our trip," Sensei said, as he blew on the soup, cupping in both hands the alumite bowl that reminded me of old-fashioned cafeteria ware.

"You studied up? Isn't that just like a teacher!" Toru responded, heartily slurping his soup.

"There are many more kinds of poisonous mushrooms than I realized," Sensei said, snaring a piece of mushroom with his chopsticks and popping it in his mouth.

"Hmmm, well . . . ," Satoru murmured. Having already drained his first bowl, he was just that moment ladling out a second serving.

"The really poisonous ones, you shouldn't even think about putting them near your mouth."

"Sensei, please stop! At least while we're eating," I pleaded, but he paid no attention to me. As usual.

"But the trouble is, it seems the *kaki-shimeji* mushroom looks exactly like the *matsutake*, and the *tsukiyotake* mushroom is indistinguishable from the *shiitake*, and so on."

Sensei's gravely serious tone caused Satoru and Toru to burst in laughter.

"Sensei, we've been collecting mushrooms for more than ten years now, and we've never once seen such strange mushrooms as that."

I now returned my chopsticks, which had been suspended in the air, to my alumite soup bowl. Unsure of whether or not Satoru and Toru had taken notice of my hesitation, I cast a furtive upward glance in their direction, but neither of them seemed to be paying any attention to me.

Satoru and Toru were both mesmerized by Sensei, who had just uttered the statement, "Actually, the woman who used to be my wife once ate a Big Laughing Gym mushroom."

"What do you mean, 'the woman who used to be my wife'?"

"I mean my wife who ran off about fifteen years ago," he said, his voice as serious as ever.

Huh? I gave out a little cry. I had assumed that Sensei's wife had died. I expected Satoru and Toru to be just as surprised, but they both seemed unfazed. As he sipped the rest of his mushroom soup, Sensei told us the following story:

My wife and I often went hiking. We usually hiked smaller mountains, places that were about an hour's train ride away. Early Sunday mornings, we'd take along a lunch my wife had packed for us and board the train, still empty at that hour. My wife had a book she loved called *Suburban Pleasure Hiking*. On its cover, there was a photo of a woman climbing a mountain with a walking stick, wearing leather hiking boots, knickerbockers, and a hat with a feather tucked into it. My wife had re-created this exact outfit—down to the walking stick—and she would wear it on our hiking trips. This is just ordinary hiking, I would say to her, You don't need to be so formal about it. But she would reply, impervious to me, It's important to dress the part. She wouldn't break character, even on a trail where people were walking around in flip-flops. She was a very hardheaded person.

This must have been when our son was in elementary school. The three of us were on one of our usual hiking trips. It was exactly the same time of year as now. It had been raining, and the mountain's fall foliage was beautiful, although many of the brilliantly colored leaves had been scattered by the rain. I was wearing sneakers and had fallen down a couple of times when they got stuck in the mud. My wife had no trouble walking in her hiking boots. But whenever I fell, she refrained from making any sort of sarcastic remark. She may have been stubborn, but she did not go in for cattiness.

After walking for a while, we took a break and each had two honeyed lemon slices. I'm not particularly fond of sour sweets, but my wife insisted that honeyed lemon went together with mountain hiking, so I didn't bother to argue. Even if I had, I doubt it would have bothered her, perhaps it would just have contributed to the subtle accumulation of anger—the way a succession of smaller waves accumulate into one big wave—that rippled throughout everyday life in unexpected places. That's just the way married life is, I suppose.

Our son liked lemon even less than I did. He put the honeyed lemon in his mouth and then stood up and walked into a thicket of trees. He liked to pick up autumn leaves from the ground. The boy had a refined sensibility. I followed him to pick up some leaves myself, but when I got closer, I saw that he was stealthily digging a hole in the ground. He hastily dug a shallow hollow, hurriedly spit out the lemon in his mouth, then swiftly filled in the hole with dirt. That's how much he disliked lemon. He wasn't the kind of child who wasted food either. My wife had raised him well.

You must really hate it, I said to him. He was a bit
startled, but then nodded silently. I'm not very fond of it
either, I said, and he smiled with relief. Our son looked a
lot like my wife when he smiled. He still looks a lot like her.
Come to think of it, he will soon be fifty years old, the same
age my wife was when she ran off.

The two of us were crouched over, busying ourselves
with collecting autumn leaves when my wife walked up. Even
though she was wearing those huge hiking boots, she didn't
make a sound. Hey there, she said behind our backs, and
we both flinched with surprise. Look what I found—a Big
Laughing Gym mushroom, she whispered in our ears.

THE FOUR OF us had quickly finished what had seemed like plenty of
mushroom soup. The combined varieties of mushrooms had mingled
together and the taste was ineffable. That had been Sensei's descrip-
tion—"ineffable." In the middle of his story, he had abruptly interrupted
himself to say, "Satoru, the soup's aroma is simply ineffable."

Satoru rolled his eyes, and Toru said, "Sensei, you sound just like a
teacher!" They urged Sensei to continue the story. What happened with
the Big Laughing Gym? Satoru asked, while Toru wondered, How did
she know it was a Big Laughing Gym?

Besides *Suburban Pleasure Hiking*, my wife had another favorite book, a little field guide to mushroom identification, like a
mushroom encyclopedia—these two books were always tucked
away in her rucksack whenever we went hiking. And, now, she
had the guide open to the page on Big Laughing Gym mushrooms, and she kept repeating, This is it! This is definitely that
kind of mushroom!

"Fine, you know it's a Big Laughing Gym, but what are
you going to do with it?" I asked her.

My wife replied, "Why, eat it, of course."

"But isn't it poisonous?" I said.

"Mom, stop it!" our son cried out.

Right at that moment—paying no mind whatsoever to the dirt on its cap—my wife popped the mushroom into her mouth. "It's a little tough to eat raw," she said, shoving a honeyed lemon slice in her mouth along with it. To this day, neither my son nor I have ever eaten another honeyed lemon slice.

What followed was quite a commotion. First our son burst into tears. "Mom is going to die!" he bawled.

"Big Laughing Gyms don't kill you," my wife comforted him, maintaining perfect composure.

In any case, we still needed to get off the mountain and go to a hospital, and I had to drag my reluctant wife back down the way we came.

Soon after, just around the time when we reached the foot of the mountain, the symptoms began to appear. Later at the hospital, the doctor commented nonchalantly that ingesting even such a small amount could bring about symptoms but, to my mind, the symptoms that she exhibited were rather remarkable.

My wife, who up until then had been so calm and collected, began to emit a sort of chortle, intermittent at first but soon growing in frequency before developing into the full-fledged so-called "laughter." They call it laughter, but there was nothing happy or cheerful about it. It sounded as though she was trying to stifle a laugh as it welled up, but for the life of her she couldn't hold back, and no matter how much she tried, her brain was unable to overcome the involuntary physical reaction—that's what kind of laugh it was. An unspeakably sinister laugh, as if at some sick joke.

Our son was terrified, I was in a panic, and my wife, her eyes filled with tears, just kept on laughing.

"Cut it out, will you?" I said, as our son whimpered faintly.

"I c-can't stop. I-It's like my throat and my f-face and my chest—n-none of them are under my c-control," my wife replied with difficulty, through her laughter.

I was irate. Why was it that she constantly needed to cause such trouble? We went hiking practically every weekend and, frankly, I didn't enjoy it very much. Neither did our son. He would probably have been just as content to stay at home, painstakingly assembling his plastic models, or to go fishing in the creek by our house, or what have you. Instead, both he and I did as we were told and got up early to wander around the hills on the outskirts of town. But that just wasn't good enough for my wife—she had to go and eat a Big Laughing Gym mushroom.

My wife was treated in the hospital, but, as the ever-nonchalant doctor said, since the mushroom's toxin was already in her bloodstream, there was really nothing they could do about it, and her condition remained more or less unchanged after he examined her. Ultimately, my wife went on laughing until that evening. We took a taxi home and I put our son, who had worn himself out crying and had fallen asleep, under the covers in his bed. I kept an eye on my still-laughing wife as she sat alone in the living room while I made us some strong green tea. My wife drank her tea, laughing, and I drank my tea, stewing in my anger.

After her symptoms subsided at last and my wife was back to normal, I started in on my lecturing. Do you have any idea how much trouble you caused for all of us, in this single day today? Oh, I was in rare form. I lectured her like I was lecturing a student. My wife listened with downcast eyes, her head hung low. She nodded at each thing I said. I'm sorry, she said over and over. When I was done, she said earnestly, "Everyone causes trouble for someone at some point in their lives."

"*I* don't cause anyone any trouble! You're the one who is a nuisance! Please refrain from extrapolating your own personal issues onto the general public," I harangued. My wife hung her head again. More than ten years later, when she ran off, I was left with a vivid recollection of her like that, eyes downcast and contrite. My wife was a difficult person, but I wasn't so different. I used to think that we complemented each other—like the saying goes: Even a cracked pot has a lid that fits. But, as it turned out, I guess I didn't fit my wife very well.

"Here, Sensei, have a drink," Toru pulled the Sawanoi saké from his rucksack. It was a 720-milliliter bottle. We had polished off the mushroom soup, but like magic, Toru produced one item after another from his bag. Dried mushrooms. Rice crackers. Dried smoked squid. Whole tomatoes. Canned bonito.

"It's quite a feast," Toru remarked. Both he and Satoru were swigging saké from paper cups and gnawing on tomatoes.

"You don't get as drunk if you eat a tomato first," they claimed.

"Sensei, do you think they'll be all right to drive?" I asked under my breath.

He replied, "One bottle between the four of us shouldn't be a problem, I guess." My stomach was already warm from the mushroom soup, and the saké warmed it even more. The tomatoes were delicious. We just bit right into them; they didn't even need salt. Apparently, they were straight from Toru's garden. He pulled out another bottle of saké from his rucksack, meaning we'd have to revise our calculations.

I heard the *ta-ra-ra-ra-ra* again. Every so often, bugs crawled underneath the newspaper we were sitting on. I could feel them moving through the paper. Various flying insects—some of them quite large—buzzed and landed around us. They seemed particularly attracted to the smoked squid and the saké. Toru paid them virtually no attention as he continued to eat and drink.

"I think you just ate a bug," Sensei pointed out to Toru, who replied with a straight face, "Mmm, delicious!"

The dried mushrooms weren't completely dehydrated, like dried *shiitake*; rather they still had a bit of moisture in them. They looked more like beef jerky. What kind of mushrooms are these? I asked.

Satoru, already red in the face, replied, "Fly agarics."

"Aren't those extremely poisonous?" Sensei asked.

"Did you look that up in your mushroom encyclopedia?" Toru said with a smirk. Instead of responding, Sensei took the mushroom field guide out of his briefcase. It was an old, well-thumbed copy, and on its cover was a mushroom that appeared to be a fly agaric, with an impressive-looking red spotted cap.

"Toru, do you know the story about these?"

"What story?"

"What they did with them in Siberia. Long ago, the chiefs of indigenous highland peoples of Siberia would ingest the fly agaric before going into battle. Fly agaric mushrooms contain constituents that induce a psychoactive trance. Once eaten, the mushroom causes an extremely agitated state characterized by ferocity and momentary bursts of tremendous strength that can persist for hours. First, the chief would eat the mushroom, and the next-highest-ranking man would drink the chief's urine. Then the next-highest-ranking man would drink the second-highest-ranking man's urine, and so on, until the mushroom's constituents were coursing through the veins of all the members of the tribe.

"Apparently, when the last man finished drinking the urine, they were prepared to do battle," Sensei concluded.

"That's a handy little mush . . . mushroom encyclopedia," Satoru said with a high-pitched laugh. He was nibbling on a shred of dried mushroom.

"Come on, you two, try some," Toru said, thrusting a dried mushroom into my hand and Sensei's hand. Sensei took a long, hard look at the mushroom. I gave it a tentative sniff. Both Toru and Satoru dissolved into senseless guffaws. Toru started to say, "You know . . . ," and Satoru roared with laughter. Once he had controlled himself, Satoru then began with, "It's like . . . ," only to have Toru cackle hysterically. The two of them tried to speak again at the same time and burst out laughing together.

The temperature had risen a bit. Even though it would soon be winter, the surrounding trees and the undergrowth beneath us provided a damp yet toasty warmth. Sensei slowly sipped his saké, intermittently nibbling on the dried mushroom.

"Do you think it's okay to eat a poisonous mushroom?" I asked. Sensei laughed. "Well, now . . . ," he replied with a charming smile.

Toru, Satoru, are these really fly agarics?

Of course not, they couldn't be.

You bet they are, the real deal.

Toru and Satoru replied at the same time. I couldn't tell which one of them had said which. Sensei was still smiling, leisurely nibbling on his mushroom.

Sensei closed his eyes as he said the words, "Cracked pot."

What's that? I asked him.

He repeated the phrase, Even a cracked pot has a lid that fits.

Tsukiko, eat the mushroom, he instructed me in his teacher's voice. Tentatively, I tried licking it, but all I could taste was dirt. Toru and Satoru were still laughing. Sensei kept smiling, looking off in the distance. Giving in, I stuffed the whole mushroom in my mouth, chewing and chewing.

We sat there drinking for another hour or so, and I noticed no real effects. We packed up our things and went back the way we came. As we walked, I felt alternately like laughing and crying. I must have been drunk. I wasn't really sure where we were going. I was definitely drunk. Satoru and Toru walked in front, with exactly the same posture and exactly the same gait. Sensei and I walked in line behind them, smiling to ourselves. Sensei, do you still love your wife, even after she ran off? I murmured.

He boomed with laughter. My wife is still an immeasurable presence in my life, he said somewhat seriously, before breaking into laughter again. I found myself surrounded by such a plethora of living things, all of them buzzing about. What on earth was I doing, wandering around a place like this?

New Year's

I SCREWED UP.

The fluorescent light in the kitchen had burnt out. It was one of those meter-long lightbulbs. I had dragged over a tall chair to stand on, in order to reach up and change the bulb. It had gone out before, and I thought I remembered how to change it, but it had been so many years that apparently I've forgotten.

No matter how much I pushed and pulled, I couldn't get the bulb out. Using a screwdriver, I then tried to remove the entire fixture, but there were these red and blue cords that attached it to the ceiling—it was constructed so that the fixture itself wouldn't come off.

That's when I yanked with all my might and it broke. The fluorescent bulb shattered all over the floor in front of the sink. Unfortunately, I was barefoot at the time so when, in a fluster, I stepped down off of the chair, I cut the sole of my foot on a shard of glass. Bright red blood gushed out. It must have cut deeper than I thought.

As I staggered into the next room to sit down, I felt a wave of dizziness. Was I anemic?

Tsukiko, do you really think you can bring on an attack of anemia just by seeing a little blood? You really are a delicate flower. That's what

Sensei would have said as he laughed at me. But Sensei had never been to my house. I had only gone to his house a few times. My eyelids fluttered as I sat there. I realized that I hadn't eaten anything since that morning. I had idled away my entire day off, spending most of it in bed. This always happened after I saw my family for the New Year's holiday.

Even though they were in the same neighborhood, I rarely visited—I just couldn't bear going back home to the boisterous house where my mother lived with my older brother and his wife and kids. At this point it wasn't about them telling me I ought to get married or quit my job. I had long ago gotten used to that particular kind of uneasiness. It was just dissatisfying in some way. It felt as if I had ordered a bunch of clothes that I had every reason to think would fit perfectly, but when I went to try them on, some were too short, while with others the hem dragged on the floor. Surprised, I would take the clothes off and hold them up against my body, only to find that they were all, in fact, the right length. Or something like that.

On the third day of the new year, when my brother and his family had gone out for a round of well-wishing, my mother made me *yudofu* for lunch. *Yudofu* had always been one of my favorite dishes. It's not the kind of thing children usually like but, since before I started elementary school, I always loved my mother's *yudofu*. In a small cup she mixes saké with soy sauce, sprinkling it with freshly shaved bonito, and then warms the cup along with the tofu in an earthenware pot. When it's hot enough, she opens the lid of the pot and a thick cloud of steam escapes. She heats the whole block of tofu without cutting it, so I can then ravage the firm cotton tofu with the tips of my chopsticks. It's no good unless you use tofu from the corner tofu shop, and they always reopen on the third, my mother chatted away as she cheerfully prepared the *yudofu* for me.

It's delicious, I said.

My mother replied with obvious pleasure, You've always loved *yudofu*, haven't you?

I can never seem to make it the same way.

That's because you use different tofu. They don't sell this kind of tofu over where you live, Tsukiko, do they?

After that, my mother fell silent. I was quiet too. Without speaking, I demolished the *yudofu*, dousing it with the saké soy sauce as I ate it. Neither of us said a word. Didn't we have anything to talk about? There must have been something. But as I tried to think of what to say, my mind went blank. You'd think we'd be close, but it was precisely because we were close that we couldn't reach each other. Forcing myself to make conversation felt like standing on a cliff, peering over the edge, about to tumble down headfirst.

Tsukiko, the way you describe it sounds like how I might feel if, after all these years, I suddenly encountered my wife who ran away. But this is your family, who lives in the same neighborhood as you do. Surely you're exaggerating a bit, aren't you? That's what Sensei might say.

He might have pointed out that my mother and I seemed similar. Nevertheless, neither one of us was any good at chitchat. So we just avoided each other's gaze until my brother and his family returned. The pale new year's light shone on the veranda, reaching all the way to the foot of the *kotatsu*. Having finished eating, I carried the earthenware pot and small plates and chopsticks into the kitchen where my mother was at the sink. Shall I dry the dishes? I asked. My mother nodded, barely raising her head and smiling awkwardly. I smiled back just as uncomfortably. We stood next to each other silently and finished up the dishes.

I WENT BACK to my apartment on the fourth of January, and for the next two days until I had to go back to work on the sixth, all I did was sleep. Unlike while I was at my mother's house, this sleep was filled with dreams.

After two days of work, I found myself off again. I wasn't really tired anymore, so I just lazed in bed. I kept a teapot and teacup within arm's reach, along with various books and magazines, and lay about while drinking tea and flipping through the pages. I ate a couple of mandarin oranges. Under the covers it was slightly warmer than my own body temperature, so I kept dozing off. Soon I'd awake again, and pick up another magazine. That was how I had forgotten to eat all day.

Back atop my unmade bed, I held toilet paper to the bleeding wound on the sole of my foot as I waited for the dizzy spell to subside. My vision seemed like a TV screen on the fritz, flickering and flashing. I lay down on my back and placed one hand over my heart. There was a slight delay between the beat of my heart and the throbbing pulse of my wound.

It had still been faintly light outside when the bulb had gone out. But now, because I was still dizzy, I couldn't tell whether or not it was twilight or if it had grown dark already.

Apples heaped in a basket by my pillow gave off their fragrance. The perfume was intensified by the chilly winter air. I always quartered my apples before peeling them but, as I lay there in a daze, I thought of how my mother used a kitchen knife to peel an apple whole, in one long curly piece. I once peeled an apple for an old boyfriend. I was never much good at cooking anyway, but even if I had been, I had no particular interest in packing lunches for him or going to his place to cook for him or inviting him over for home-cooked meals. I was always afraid that doing so would put me in a compromising position—trapped in the kitchen, so to speak. And I didn't want him to think that he was the one who had put me there either. It may not have mattered whether or not I found myself trapped there, but somehow I couldn't manage to make light of it.

When I peeled the apple, my boyfriend was astonished. So, you can peel an apple, huh? That's how he said it.

I think I can manage, I replied.

Is that so?

Yes, it is.

Not long after this exchange, this boyfriend and I drifted apart.
Neither one of us actually initiated it; we simply stopped calling each
other. It wasn't that I lost interest. The days just went by without us seeing each other.

You're a bit aloof, a friend told me. He called me several times, to
ask for advice. "How does Tsukiko really feel about me?" he would ask.
Why didn't you ever call him? He was waiting for you.

My friend fixed her gaze on me. I was bewildered. Why didn't he
ask me directly, instead of going to my friend? I simply couldn't com-
prehend it. When I said as much to my friend, she just sighed. Tsukiko,
she murmured, being in love makes people uncertain. Don't you know
what that's like?

But as far as I was concerned, that wasn't the point. I couldn't help
but think it had been misguided of him to go to my friend—a third
party—when he ought to have brought his uncertainty to me, the one
who it involved.

I'm sorry for putting you in that situation. It's illogical that he
went to you with this. I apologized, but now my friend drew an even
deeper sigh.

Illogical? What does logic have to do with this?

At that point, it had already been more than three months since I
had seen this boyfriend. My friend had gone on at length about this and
that aspect of my relationship with him, but I had only been half listening. I was pretty sure that I wasn't very good at this whole love thing.
And if being in love required so much effort, then I wasn't sure I wanted
to be a part of it anyway. That friend ended up marrying that boyfriend
a little more than six months later.

My DIZZINESS PASSED. I could now make out the ceiling. The lightbulb
in this room hadn't burnt out, it just wasn't turned on yet. Outside it
was dark. Cold air came in through the window. It was suddenly much

chillier now that the sun was gone. Lazing in bed all day had brought up memories of the past. My foot wasn't really bleeding anymore. I put on a large Band-Aid, then put on socks and slippers, and cleaned up the mess in front of the sink.

The glass shards glimmered slightly in the light reflected from the now-illuminated bulb in the next room. I had, in fact, been very much in love with that boyfriend. I guess I should have called him back then. I had wanted to at the time, but the prospect of hearing his cold voice on the other end of the line had frozen me in place. I hadn't known that he felt the same way. By the time I found out, my feelings had already been oddly distorted, squashed down into the furthest reaches of my heart. I had dutifully attended the wedding of my friend and my boyfriend. Someone had made a toast, saying their love was fated in the stars.

"A love fated in the stars." As I sat there, watching the happy couple seated on the wedding platform and listening to the toast, I remember thinking to myself there wasn't a chance in a million that I would ever encounter "a love fated in the stars."

I had a craving for an apple so I took one from the basket. I tried to peel it the way my mother did. Partway around, the skin broke off. I suddenly burst into tears, which took me by surprise. I was cutting an apple, not chopping onions—why should there be tears? I kept crying in between bites of the apple. The crisp sound of my chewing alternated with the *plink, plink* of my tears as they fell into the stainless steel sink. Standing there, I busied myself with eating and crying.

I PUT ON a heavy coat and left the apartment. I'd had this coat for years. Deep green, worn, and fuzzy, it was still a very warm coat. I always felt colder than usual after a crying jag. I finished my apple and soon had enough of sitting in my apartment, shivering. I put on a loose-fitting red sweater, which I'd also had for years, over brown wool pants. I changed into bulky socks, slid on thick-soled sneakers and, lastly, gloves, and went out the door.

The three stars of Orion's belt were clearly visible in the sky. I walked straight ahead. I tried to maintain a brisk pace, and I started to warm up after I'd walked for a while. A dog barked at me from somewhere, and instantly I burst into tears. I would soon turn forty, yet here I was acting like a little girl. I kept walking, swinging my arms like a child. When I came across an empty can, I kicked it. I grabbed and pulled at the tall, withered grass on the side of the street. Several people on bicycles rushed past me, coming from the station. One of them didn't have his light on, and when we almost collided, he yelled at me. Tears welled up anew. I had the urge to sit down right there and sob, but it was too cold for that.

I had completely regressed. I stood in front of a bus stop. After waiting ten minutes, there was still no bus. I checked the bus schedule and saw that the last bus had already come and gone. I felt even more lonesome. I stamped my feet. I could not get warm. A grown woman would know how to get warm in a situation like this. But, for the moment, I was a child and helpless.

I decided to head toward the station. The familiar streets seemed alienating somehow. I felt just like a child who had tarried on her way, and now it was dark out and the streets that led back home seemed unrecognizable.

Sensei, I whispered. Sensei, I can't find my way home.

But Sensei wasn't here. I wondered where he was, on a night like this. It made me realize that I had never called Sensei on the telephone. We always met by chance, then would happen to go for a walk together. Or I would show up at his house, and we'd end up drinking together. Sometimes a month would go by without seeing or speaking to each other. In the past, if I didn't hear from a boyfriend or if we didn't have a date for a month, I'd be seized with worry. I'd wonder if, during that time, he'd completely vanished from my life, or become a stranger to me.

Sensei and I didn't see each other very often. It stands to reason, since we weren't a couple. Yet even when we were apart, Sensei never seemed far away. Sensei would always be Sensei. On a night like this, I knew he was out there somewhere.

Feeling more and more forlorn, I began to sing. I started out with "How lovely, spring has come to the Sumida River," but it was completely out of keeping with the cold night. I racked my brain for a winter song but couldn't call any to mind. At last I remembered "The silver-white mountains, bathed in morning light," a ski song. It didn't quite fit my mood but I didn't have much choice since I couldn't come up with any other winter songs, and I went on singing.

Is it snow or is it mist, fluttering in the air,
Oh, as I rush down the hill, down the hill.

I remembered the words clearly. Not just the first verse but the second verse as well. I was surprised that I could resurrect such lines as "Oh what fun, bounding with such skill." I was feeling a little better so I moved on to the third verse, but no matter how I tried, the last part would not come back to me. I could remember "The trees above and the white snow beneath" but not the last four bars.

I stopped and stood there in the darkness, trying to think. Every so often someone would walk by from the direction of the station. They avoided me as I stood rooted to the spot. And when I started singing snatches of the third verse under my breath, they gave me an even wider berth.

Still unable to remember the last words, I felt like crying again. My feet started walking of their own accord as my tears started flowing on their own as well. Tsukiko. I heard my name but didn't turn around. I figured it must have been in my head. After all, Sensei wouldn't very well just appear here.

Tsukiko. I heard someone call my name again.

I turned around this time, only to see Sensei standing there with his perfect posture. He was wearing a lightweight but warm-looking coat and carrying his briefcase, as always.

Sensei, what are you doing here?

Taking a walk. It's a lovely evening.

Just to be sure that it really was Sensei, I surreptitiously pinched the back of my hand. It hurt. This was the first time in my life that I realized people actually did such a thing—pinched themselves to make sure they weren't dreaming.

Sensei, I called out. He was a little ways away from me, so I called out softly.

Tsukiko, he replied, enunciating my name.

We stood there for a moment, facing each other in the darkness, and I no longer felt like crying. Which was a relief, since I had started to worry that my tears would never stop. And I didn't even want to imagine what Sensei might say to me if he saw me crying.

Tsukiko, the last verse, it's "Oh, the mountain calls to me," Sensei said.

What?

The words to the ski song. I used to ski a bit myself back in the day.

Sensei and I began walking side by side. We headed toward the station. Satoru's bar is closed on holidays, I said.

Sensei nodded, still facing forward. It would be good for us to go somewhere else for a change. Tsukiko. I just realized this will be our first drink together this year. That's right—happy new year, Tsukiko.

Next to Satoru's place was another bar with a red paper lantern hanging out front. We went in and sat down with our coats still on. We ordered draft beer and drained our glasses in one gulp. Tsukiko, you remind me of something, Sensei said after his first quaff. What is it . . . ? Hmm, it's on the tip of my tongue.

I ordered *yudofu* and Sensei ordered yellowtail teriyaki. A-ha, I've got it! With your green coat, red sweater, and brown pants, you look like a Christmas tree! Sensei said in a slightly high-pitched voice.

But it's already New Year's, I replied.

Did you spend Christmas with your boyfriend, Tsukiko? Sensei asked.

I did not.

Do you have a boyfriend, Tsukiko?

Yeah, I've got one or two, or ten boyfriends, even.

I see, I see.

We soon switched to saké. I picked up the bottle of hot saké and filled Sensei's cup. I felt a sudden rush of warmth in my body, and felt the tears well up once again. But I didn't cry. It's always better to drink than to cry. Sensei, happy new year. I wish you all the best in the coming year, I said in one breath.

Sensei laughed. Tsukiko, what a lovely greeting. Well done! Sensei patted me on the head as he complimented me. With his hand still on my head, I took a long sip of saké.

Karma

....

I UNEXPECTEDLY RAN into Sensei as I was walking along the street.

I had been lazing about in bed until past noon. Work had been extremely busy for the past month. It was always close to midnight by the time I got home. For days on end, I would hastily scrub my face before falling into bed, without bothering with my nighttime bath. Even on weekends, I almost always went in to the office. I had been eating terribly and, as a result, I looked drawn and haggard. I'm a bit of a gourmand, so when I'm not able to take the time to indulge my tastes as I please, I begin to lose a certain vitality, as was reflected in my pallid complexion.

Then at last on Friday—yesterday—I had successfully gotten through a major portion of the work. For the first time in what felt like ages, I slept in on Saturday morning. After having a good lie-in, I filled the bath to the brim with hot water and took a magazine in with me. I washed my hair and immersed myself countless times in the hot water, into which I had trickled a wonderfully scented potion, occasionally stepping out to cool off, all the while perusing about halfway through the magazine. I must have spent nearly two hours in the bathroom.

I drained the water from the bath and quickly scrubbed the tub, and then I pranced about my apartment, naked except for a towel twisted atop my head. It was one of those moments when I think to myself, *I'm glad to be alone.* I opened the refrigerator and took out a bottle of mineral water, poured half of it into a glass, and gulped it down. It made me think about how I had hated mineral water when I was younger. In my twenties, I had traveled to France with a girlfriend of mine, and we had gone into a café to get something to drink. I just wanted plain, regular water, but when I ordered "Water," they brought out mineral water. I was so parched and hoping to quench my thirst, but the moment I swallowed it down, I choked and nearly threw up. Yet I was so thirsty. And here was water, right in front of me. Yet this water—with bubbles springing up from the carbonation—was a bitter mouthful. Even had I wanted to drink it, my throat would reject it. But since I didn't know enough French to say, "I would prefer still water rather than water with gas," I forced my friend to share with me the lemonade that she had ordered. It was terribly sweet—awful, really. That was before I was in the habit of slaking my thirst with beer instead of water.

I started to enjoy carbonated water when I was in my mid-thirties, around the time I started drinking highballs and *shochu* with soda and the like. At some point I started keeping a few tall green bottles of Wilkinson soda water in the fridge. For that matter, I also keep a few bottles of Wilkinson ginger ale, for the occasional times when a friend who doesn't really drink stops by. In general—with clothes or food or gadgets—I have no particular brand loyalty, but when it comes to soda water, the only kind I drink is Wilkinson soda water. The main reason is probably because the liquor store two minutes away happens to carry Wilkinson brand soda water. That may seem like happenstance, but if I were to move and there were no liquor store in my new neighborhood, or if there were one and it didn't carry Wilkinson's superior products, then I would probably no longer bother keeping soda water around at all. That's the extent of my partiality.

Often when I was alone, such were the contents of my head. Random thoughts about the Wilkinson brand or a European trip from the distant past would bubble up in my mind, like effervescent carbonation, and continue their wistful proliferation. I was still naked, standing idly in front of the full-length mirror. I had a habit of acting as though I were having a conversation with someone beside me—with the me who was not really right there beside me—as if to validate these random effervescences. What I see in the mirror is not my own lithe, naked body, more than necessarily subject to gravity—I'm not speaking to the me who is visible there, but rather to an invisible version of myself that I sense hovering somewhere in the room.

I stayed in my apartment until evening, passing the time leisurely reading a book. At one point I felt sleepy again and napped for about half an hour. When I awoke, I opened the curtains to see that it was completely dark out. It was early February, and according to the lunar calendar the first day of spring had passed, but the days were still short. I find something quite carefree about the days around the winter solstice, when the daylight is so brief it seems like it's chasing you. Knowing that it will soon be dark anyway, I'm able to steel myself against that inevitable sense of regret brought on by the evening twilight. This time of year, rather, with its prolonged nightfall—it's not dark yet, soon but not quite dark yet—seemed to play tricks on me. The moment after I realized it was dark, I would feel a surge of loneliness.

That's why I left the apartment. Out on the street, I wanted to make sure that I wasn't the only one here, that I wasn't the only one feeling lonely. But this wasn't the kind of thing you could tell just by looking at the passersby. The harder I tried to see, the less sure I was about anything.

It was then that I unexpectedly ran into Sensei.

· · ·

"TSUKIKO, MY BUTT hurts," Sensei blurted out as we stood there together.

Huh? Shocked, I checked his expression and, rather than pained, he looked quite impassive. What happened to your butt? I asked, and Sensei frowned slightly.

"A young lady mustn't use a word like 'butt.'"

Before I could say, Well, what the hell word should I use then? Sensei added, "There are various other options such as 'backside' or 'posterior' and so forth."

He went on, "Indeed, it's a shame what limited vocabularies young people have nowadays."

Without replying to him, I laughed, and Sensei laughed too.

"So then, don't let's go to Satoru's place tonight."

Shocked once again, I thought, *Huh?* Seeing my reaction, Sensei nodded lightly in my direction.

"If I appear to be in pain, Satoru will worry. I have no intention of causing someone concern while I'm having a drink."

I was about to ask, In that case, why bother going for a drink at all?

"But you know what they say: 'Even a chance meeting is the result of a karmic connection.'"

Do you think you and I have a karmic connection? I asked.

"Tsukiko, do you know what that means, a 'karmic connection'?" Sensei asked in return.

Something to do with chance? I ventured after thinking for a moment.

Sensei shook his head with furrowed brows. "Not chance, but rather, destiny. Transmigration of the soul."

I see, I replied. I, uh . . . Japanese class was not my best subject.

"That's because you didn't study hard enough," Sensei said judgmentally. "Tsukiko, the idea of karmic destiny comes from the Buddhist concept that all living things are reincarnated again and again."

Sensei stood in front of the *odenya* that was next door to Satoru's place before we ducked inside. Looking closely, I noticed that Sensei's torso was indeed slightly off-kilter as he walked. I wondered how much his butt—ahem, his backside—was hurting him. I couldn't tell anything from his expression.

"Hot saké, please," Sensei called out, and I ordered a bottle of beer. We were promptly served, a hot saké bottle and a half-liter bottle of beer, along with a saké cup and a beer glass. We each poured into the appropriate vessels for ourselves and said cheers.

"So, in other words, a karmic connection refers to a bond from a previous life."

A previous life? I said, slightly raising my voice. We were connected in a previous life, you and I?

"Everyone's connected somehow, perhaps," Sensei replied serenely, taking care as he poured saké from the bottle to his cup. A young man seated next to us at the counter was staring at Sensei and me. I had caught his attention when I raised my voice a moment ago. The guy had three piercings in his ear. He wore gold studs in two of the holes and, in the first hole, a dangling earring that swayed with a particular shimmer.

I'd like hot saké too, I called out my order to the counter and then asked, Sensei, do you believe in past lives? The guy next to us seemed to be eavesdropping.

"Sort of." Sensei's response was unexpected. I thought he would say something like, Tsukiko, what about you, do you believe in past lives? You know, it's awfully sentimental.

"Past lives, or fate, that is."

Daikon, *tsumire*, and beef tendons, please, Sensei ordered.

Not to be outdone, I followed with *Chikuwabu*, *konnyaku* noodles, and I'll also have some *daikon*. The young man next to us asked for *kombu* and *hanpen*. We left off our conversation about fate and past lives while we focused on eating our *oden* for the moment. Sensei, still off-kilter, brought to his mouth the daikon that he had cut into bite-size pieces with his chopsticks, while I hunched forward a little to nibble on my piece of daikon.

The saké and the *oden* are so delicious, I said. Sensei patted me lightly on the head. Lately, I had noticed that, from time to time, Sensei had taken to this gentle gesture.

"It's nice to see someone who enjoys eating," he said as he patted my head.

Shall we order a little more, Sensei?

Good idea.

We chatted as we ordered. The young man beside us was quite red in the face. What appeared to be three empty saké bottles were lined up in front of him, along with an empty glass, so he must have had beer too. He radiated drunkenness, as if his heavy breathing could reach all the way over to us.

"You two, just what are you?" He blurted out suddenly. He had barely touched the *kombu* and *hanpen* on his plate. Pouring saké into his cup from a fourth bottle, he exhaled in our direction, his breath reeking of alcohol. His earring glimmered brilliantly.

"What do you mean by that?" Sensei replied, pouring from his own bottle.

"That's a pretty good setup, you know, for you two," he said with a smirk. There was something peculiar about his laugh though. It was as if he had somehow swallowed a frog and now he couldn't seem to laugh from his gut anymore—his strangely menacing laugh sounded like it was caught in his throat.

"And what do you mean by that?" Sensei earnestly asked him in return.

"You're much older than she is but still, you're all cozy together."

Sensei nodded magnanimously, as if to say, *Ah, yes*, and looked straight before him. You could almost hear a slapping sound at that moment. *I do not deign to speak to the likes of you.* Sensei may not have uttered the words, but it was clear that was what he was thinking. I sensed it, and the guy must have sensed it too.

"It's perverted, really. Act your age!" He seemed to realize that Sensei was not going to respond to him anymore, yet, nevertheless, that only encouraged his vehemence.

"Are you doing it with this old man?" he said to me, looking past Sensei. His voice echoed throughout the *odenya*. I glanced at Sensei but, of course, he was not going to break his expression over such a comment.

"How many times a month do you do it, huh?"

"Now, Yasuda, that's enough," the owner of the *odenya* tried to cut him off. The young man was considerably drunker than he initially appeared to be. His body was twitching as he swayed backward and forward. If Sensei hadn't been sitting between us, I surely would have slapped the guy in the face.

"Shuttup!" He now turned to shout at the owner, and tried to douse him in the face with the saké in his cup. But he was so drunk that his aim was off, and he spilled most of it on his own pants instead.

"Fuck!" he shouted again, using a towel the owner had handed him to wipe off his pants as well as the area around him. Then suddenly he fell flat on the counter, and immediately started to snore.

"Yasuda's been a terrible drunk lately," the owner said to us, waving one hand and bowing his head.

I see. I nodded vaguely, but Sensei didn't nod at all, he simply said, in the same tone of voice as always, "Another bottle of hot saké, please."

"Tsukiko, I'm terribly sorry."

The young man was still passed out on the counter and snoring. The owner had tried repeatedly to shake him awake, to no avail. If he wakes up, you see, I'm sure he'll go right home, the owner said to us before going to take a table's order.

"That must have been awfully unpleasant for you, Tsukiko. I'm terribly sorry."

Please don't apologize for him, Sensei, I was about to say, but I held my tongue. I was livid with anger. Not for myself, that is, but for Sensei being put in the position to make such a ridiculous apology.

I really wish this guy would hurry up and leave, I whispered, gesturing to him with my chin. But he refused to budge, and just kept right on with his absurdly loud snoring.

"That thing really sparkles, doesn't it?" Sensei said.

Huh? I muttered, and Sensei pointed at the guy's earring with a grin and a snicker. You're right, it certainly does, I replied, somewhat dumbfounded. There were times when Sensei really puzzled me. I ordered another bottle of saké too, and drank in its warmth. Sensei just kept on with his chuckling. What could he be laughing at? Dejected, I went to the bathroom and did my business vigorously. I felt a little better, and by the time I sat back down next to Sensei, I had settled down a bit more.

"Tsukiko, look, look at this." Sensei held out his hand and gently uncurled his fingers to reveal something sparkly, there in his palm.

What is that?

"Just what you think—look, it's what was on his ear." Sensei's gaze trailed over to the still-snoring young man. My eyes followed his, and I saw that the sparkliest jangle that had been hanging from the guy's ear was gone. The two gold studs were still there, but at the edge of his earlobe there was nothing but an empty hole that seemed to gape a bit now.

Sensei, you took it?

"I stole it." His expression was perfectly innocent.

Now, why would you do that? I reproached him, but Sensei was quite unperturbed. He shook his head.

"The author Hyakken Uchida wrote something like this," Sensei started in.

If I recall, there is a short story called "The Amateur Pickpocket."

There's a fellow who gets boorishly rude and impolite when he drinks, and he always wears a gold chain that dangles from his neck. His rudeness itself is bothersome enough, but the sight of this chain becomes more and more offensive to another fellow, so he steals it. Just like that, he takes it. Do not assume that because the boor was drunk it was an easy thing to do—the one who stole it was drunk himself, so it was an equal task.

"That's the gist of it. Hyakken, he's really quite good." Now that I thought about it, Sensei used to always wear this same ingenuous expression during Japanese class. I remembered it well.

Is that why you stole it? I asked.

Sensei nodded vigorously. "You could say I was following after Hyakken."

Are you familiar with Hyakken, Tsukiko? I figured Sensei would ask me this, but he did not. I thought I might have heard his name before, but I wasn't sure. The logic of the story was nonsense, though. Drunk or not, it was wrong to steal. Yet the scenario was strangely apt. And what made sense about it seemed particularly fitting to Sensei.

"Tsukiko, I didn't do this in order to teach that fellow a lesson. I stole the earring because I found him annoying and I wanted to. Make no mistake about it."

Oh, I won't, I replied warily, and gulped down my saké. We each finished off another bottle, then paid our separate bills, as usual, and left the *odenya*.

THE MOON SHONE brightly. It was almost full.

Sensei . . . Sensei, do you ever feel lonely? The question popped out as the two of us walked side by side, both facing forward.

"I felt lonely when I hurt my butt," Sensei replied, still looking ahead.

That's right, what happened to your butt—er, I mean, your backside?

"As I was putting on my pants, my foot got caught and I fell over. I landed very hard on my butt."

I couldn't stifle my laughter. Sensei laughed a little too.

"I suppose it wasn't loneliness that I felt. Physical pain inspires the worst kind of helplessness."

Sensei, do you like mineral water? I moved on to another question.

"This conversation is jumping around, isn't it? Let's see, well, I've always enjoyed Wilkinson brand soda water."

Really? Is that so? I replied, still facing forward.

The moon was high in the sky, with a few thin clouds. The first signs of spring were still a ways away, yet spring felt closer at hand than when we had entered the *odenya*.

What are you going to do with that earring? I asked.

Sensei thought for a moment before answering. "I think I'll keep it in my bureau. I'll take it out sometimes for amusement."

In the bureau where you keep the railway teapots? I asked.

Sensei nodded gravely. "That's correct. In the bureau where I keep commemorative items."

Is tonight a night to commemorate?

"It's been a long time since I stole something."

So then, Sensei, when did you learn how to steal?

"In a previous life, sort of," Sensei said, letting out a little chuckle.

Sensei and I strolled along. There was a faint promise of spring in the night air. The moon glimmered in gold.

The Cherry
Blossom Party, Part 1

I WAS APPREHENSIVE when Sensei announced, "I received a postcard from Ms. Ishino."

Ms. Ishino was still the art teacher at our high school. When I was a student, she had probably still been in her mid-thirties. She always used to whisk through the corridors wearing her artist's smock and with her luxuriantly black and wavy hair pulled to the back. Slender, she seemed to brim with vigor. Equally popular with girls as well as boys, her classroom after school would always be chock-full of the quirky and peculiar students who were in the art club.

Ms. Ishino would be shut up in the art prep room, and when the aroma of coffee drifted out to the classroom, the art students knocked on her door.

"What is it?" Ms. Ishino would answer in her husky voice.

"Please, Ms. Ishino, let us have a coffee klatch," one of the art students would say through the door. He spoke in a deliberately bewildered tone.

"All right, all right," Ms. Ishino would say, opening the door and handing over the entire siphon full of coffee to the students. Those allowed to partake in the coffee klatch were the club president and vice president, along with several other seniors. Lowerclassmen had not yet earned the right. Ms. Ishino would emerge from the prep room to drink coffee with them, clasping in both hands an oversized Mashiko-ware mug that she had fired herself in a friend's kiln. Then she would straighten her shoulders a bit and take a look around at the art club students' work. She would sit back down in a chair and finish her coffee. She never added cream. Students would bring their own non-dairy creamer or packets of sugar, because Ms. Ishino always took her coffee black.

A classmate of mine who was in the art club had raptly proclaimed, Someday I hope to be like Ms. Ishino ... So I had peeked into her classroom a few times out of curiosity. Nobody seemed to care if people who weren't in the art club hung out there too. The place was warm, reeking of paint thinner and a hint of cigarette smoke.

"She's so cool, isn't she?" my friend would say, and I'd mumble and nod, Yeah, well. But the truth was that I hated things like "handmade Mashiko-ware." I didn't feel particularly strongly one way or another about Ms. Ishino's appearance, just her big hand-thrown coffee mug. I didn't hold anything against Mashiko-ware in and of itself, per se.

I took Ms. Ishino's art class my first year in high school, but that was it. I have a vague memory of doing charcoal sketches of plaster figures and watercolor still lifes. My grades were below average. While we were students there, Ms. Ishino had married the social studies teacher. She was probably in her mid-fifties now.

"It's an invitation to the cherry-blossom-viewing party," Sensei said a few moments later.

I see, I replied. The cherry blossom party?

"It's an annual event. They do it every year, a few days before school starts in April, on the embankment in front of the school. Tsukiko, how would you like to join me at this year's cherry blossom party?" Sensei asked.

I see, I repeated myself. Cherry blossom parties are nice. But there was nothing nice about the tone of my voice. Sensei, however, paid no attention as he stared fixedly at the postcard.

"Ms. Ishino has always had such fine penmanship," he said. Then Sensei carefully unzipped his briefcase and slid the postcard into one of the compartments. I watched absentmindedly as he zipped it back shut again.

"Don't forget, it's on April 7," Sensei reminded me as he waved from the bus stop.

I'll try not to forget, I replied, as if I were a student again. It was somewhat of a careless phrase, insecure and childish.

No MATTER HOW many times I heard it, I could not get used to the name Mr. Matsumoto. That was, of course, what everyone called Sensei. His full name was Mr. Harutsuna Matsumoto. Apparently the other teachers called each other "Mr." or "Ms." Mr. Matsumoto. Mr. Kyogoku. Ms. Honda. Mr. Nishikawahara. Ms. Ishino. And so on.

Even though Sensei had invited me, I had no interest in going to the cherry blossom party. I figured I would get out of it by making some excuse about being very busy at work or something. But the day of the party, Sensei showed up outside my apartment to pick me up. It was very unusual behavior for Sensei. Unusual, but nevertheless, there he was—standing tall, wearing a spring jacket, and carrying his briefcase.

"Tsukiko, did you bring something to sit on?" He stood outside my building as he asked me various things. He made no move to come up to my place on the second floor. When I saw Sensei's smiling face, as he waited for me with complete assurance, I simply couldn't bring myself to make excuses. Resigned, I hastily stuffed a stiff plastic sheet into a bag, threw on whatever clothes I found randomly scattered about, and slipped into the same sneakers that I had worn on the mushroom hunt with Satoru and Toru (and had yet to clean off) before bounding down the stairs.

The scene on the school's embankment was already in full swing. Current teachers along with retired teachers, as well as a number of former students, had laid mats and sheets over the entire bank, lined up bottles of saké and beer, and set out food they had brought, and everyone was laughing merrily. It was difficult to tell where the center of the party was. After Sensei and I put down our sheet and greeted the people around us, still more people continued to arrive, each of them laying out mats they had brought. The cherry blossom party guests seemed to steadily spread out, like a plant's leaves unfurling as its bud blooms.

The space between Sensei and me was quickly filled by an elderly gentleman, Mr. Settsu, and then the space between Mr. Settsu and me was occupied by a young teacher, Ms. Makita. She was joined by other former students—two women named Shibasaki and Kayama and a man named Onda—but I soon lost track of who was whom.

Before I knew it, Sensei was standing next to Ms. Ishino, talking animatedly as he drank saké. He was holding a skewer of chicken with teriyaki sauce that he had bought at a storefront in the shopping district. Any other time, Sensei would stubbornly insist on salted skewers when he ate yakitori. But apparently he was capable of flexibility under certain circumstances, I thought, growing reproachful as I sipped saké by myself in a corner.

FROM ATOP THE embankment, the schoolyard grounds seemed to reflect back in white. The school was quiet, the new term having not yet begun. The buildings and the schoolyard were unchanged since I had been a student here. But the cherry trees that were planted all around had grown considerably taller.

Suddenly I heard someone say, "Hey, Omachi, not married yet?" and I glanced up. Without my noticing, a middle-aged man had come to sit near me. Looking me in the eye now, he took a sip of saké from his paper cup.

"I've been married and divorced seventeen times, but I'm single now," I quipped in response. His face was familiar but I couldn't place him. He was dumbstruck at first but then he let out a chuckle.

"Well, then, that's quite a remarkable life you've had."

"Not at all."

Deep within his laughing face, there was a faint semblance of what he had looked like in high school. That's right, we had definitely been in the same class. I remembered how when he laughed his face seemed to change completely from when he was in repose. But what was his name? It was on the tip of my tongue, yet I couldn't recall it.

"As for me, I was only married and divorced the one time," he said, still chuckling.

I had drunk about half of the saké in my paper cup. There was a flower petal floating in it.

"It wasn't easy for either one of us." Even through his quiet laughter, a warmth showed in his expression. I remembered his name—Takashi Kojima. We had been in the same homeroom for our first two years in high school. Both of us had similar numbers for attendance call, so that when they assigned seats according to these numbers, we were always seated near each other.

"I'm sorry for making such a strange joke before," I apologized.

Kojima just shook his head and laughed again.

"Omachi, you were always like that."

"Like what?"

"The type who would say something outlandish with a totally straight face."

Was that right? I never would have thought of myself as the type who made jokes or witty remarks. I was more likely the type who spent recess in a quiet corner of the schoolyard, sometimes tossing back an errant ball.

"Kojima, what do you do now?"

"I work in an office. And you?"

"Me too."

"Really?"

"Really."

There was a slight breeze. Even though the cherry blossoms were not yet in full bloom, every now and then the wind would catch one or two petals and send them scattering.

"So, you know, I was married to Ayuko," Takashi Kojima muttered after a brief silence.

"You were?"

Ayuko was the girl who had said she wanted to grow up to be like Ms. Ishino, the same classmate who had brought me to the art room after school. Now that I thought about it, Ayuko *was* sort of like Ms. Ishino. She was petite and full of energy, but she could also appear quite timid. She must have been aware of it too. It was this quality that attracted lots of boys. Ayuko was always getting "love letters" or "pickups." But she never responded to any of them. At least not openly. There were rumors that she was dating a college boy or a businessman, but whenever she and I would walk home together from school, getting soft-serve ice cream or just chatting, I never had the slightest impression any of that was true.

"I had no idea," I said to Kojima now.

"Hardly anyone did."

Kojima said that they had gotten married while they were still students at university, but that they had split up after three years.

"That's a pretty short marriage."

"Ayuko insisted on getting married, she didn't want us just to live together."

Kojima had failed his entrance exams and started university a year later, so Ayuko had entered the workforce a year before him. She fell in love with her boss and, after much ado, they finally got divorced. Kojima relayed the story dispassionately.

Now that I thought about it, Kojima and I had gone on a date once. It was during the last term of our junior year in high school, I remembered. We went to a movie. We met up at a bookstore, walked to the cinema, and used tickets that Kojima had bought in advance. "I can pay you," I had said, but Kojima had replied, "It's okay, I got the tickets from my brother."

I don't think I realized that Kojima probably didn't have a brother until the next day.

After we saw the movie, we walked through a park, talking about our reaction to the film. Kojima had been rather impressed by a trick that was employed in the film. I, on the other hand, had been rather impressed by the various hats worn by the lead actress. We came upon a kiosk selling crepes, and Kojima asked if I wanted one. When I answered no, he had grinned and said, "Good, I'm not one for sweets anyway." Instead, we got hot dogs and *yakisoba* that we washed down with colas.

And now I find out after graduation that, in fact, Kojima is quite fond of sweets.

"How is Ayuko?" I asked.

"She's fine," he nodded. "She married her boss, and they live in a three-story prefab home, it seems."

"Prefab, huh?" I murmured, and Kojima repeated, "Yup, prefab."

A strong breeze blew up, and the petals swirled around the two of us.

"So, you never married?" he asked me.

No—I mean, I don't know anything about prefab housing, I replied. Kojima laughed. We drained our cups of saké, petals and all.

"Tsukiko, come here," Sensei called. Ms. Ishino was beckoning me as well. There was a hint of excitement in Sensei's voice. I pretended not to hear him, to be engrossed in conversation with Kojima.

Even when Kojima said, "Someone's calling you," I only made a vague reply. Kojima's cheeks were flushed red. I never really liked Mr. Matsumoto, he said quietly. What about you?

I don't really remember him, I said, and Kojima nodded. That's right, you were always a million miles away. Here in body, not in spirit, or so they say.

Sensei and Ms. Ishino beckoned me for the umpteenth time. Right at that moment I happened to be facing in their direction as I tried to fix my windblown hair. I couldn't help but catch Sensei's gaze.

"Tsukiko, come over here with us," Sensei said loudly. It was the same tone of voice that I recognized from the classroom in my high school days. His tone was different when we sat next to each other, drinking together. I turned my back to him, sulkily.

"You know, I had a bit of a crush on Ms. Ishino," Kojima said blithely. His cheeks were now an even deeper shade of crimson.

"Yeah, Ms. Ishino sure was popular," I said, trying not to sound emotional.

"Ayuko was really crazy about her."

"Yeah."

"I guess that's why I fell for her too."

That was just like Kojima, to fall in line. I poured some saké into his cup. Kojima gave a little sigh and took a tiny sip.

"She's as pretty as ever."

"She is." No emotion. Or so I tried to tell myself.

"It's hard to believe she must be in her fifties."

"You're right." Must not get emotional.

Sensei was engaged in a lively conversation with Ms. Ishino (of that I was sure, despite the fact that my back was turned to them). I no longer heard him calling my name. The sun was starting to set. There were numerous lanterns lit. The cherry blossom party grew merrier and merrier as here and there people were breaking into song.

"Do you want to go somewhere else for a drink?" Kojima asked.

Right next to us, a group of students who had graduated a few years before us started singing, "I used to run after rabbits on that mountain."

Hmm, what do you think? I murmured. But the same moment one of the women's voices rang out in a fine vibrato, and Kojima leaned forward, saying, What? I missed that.

What do you think? I repeated, loudly this time. He then pulled his face back and smiled.

"Now I remember, you always used to say things like that—'What do you think?' Or 'I'm not sure . . .' Was that right?"

"And then you say that with such conviction."

You are convinced of your uncertainty! Kojima said amiably.

"Shall we go?" I said, drawing out the words.

"Let's get out of here. Let's get a drink somewhere else."

It was completely dark, and the group beside us had finished singing the third verse of "My Hometown." Every now and then, amid the cacophony, snippets of Sensei and Ms. Ishino's conversation reached my ears. Sensei's voice sounded somewhat more strident than when he spoke to me, while Ms. Ishino's still had that familiar huskiness, although I couldn't quite make out what they were saying, only the interrogatives and inflections at the end of their sentences.

"Let's go," I said, standing up. I brushed the sand off the plastic sheet and carelessly crumpled it up while Kojima stared at me.

"Omachi, you're a bit of a brute, huh?" he asked.

Yes, I am, I replied, and Kojima laughed again. He had a warm-hearted laugh. I peered through the darkness in Sensei's direction but I couldn't see very well.

Let me have a go, Kojima said as he took the sheet from my hands and neatly folded it back up for me.

Where to? I asked as Kojima and I turned away from our places at the cherry blossom party and started down the stairs that led from the embankment to the street.

The Cherry Blossom Party, Part 2

TAKASHI KOJIMA TOOK me to a cozy little bar that was located on the underground level of a building.

"I didn't know there was a bar like this so close to school," I said, and Kojima nodded.

"Of course, I never came here when we were high school students," he said earnestly. The bartender laughed at his comment. The bartender was a woman. Her hair, faintly flecked with gray, was smoothed back perfectly, and she wore a crisply ironed white shirt with a garçon-style black apron.

Kojima introduced her as Maeda, the owner of the bar, and as she set out a plate of edamame, she asked in a soft, low voice, "How many years has it been since you started coming here, Kojima?"

"Hmm, I came here a lot with Ayuko."

"Ah, yes."

That meant that he must have been a longtime regular. Because if he came here with Ayuko, then they must have been here before they had broken up, which meant that Kojima had been frequenting this bar for more than twenty years.

Kojima turned to me and asked, "Omachi, are you hungry?"

"I'm a little hungry," I replied.

"Me too," Kojima said.

"The food's tasty here," he added, taking a menu from Maeda.

I'll let you decide, I said, and he turned his gaze to the menu.

Cheese omelet. Green salad. Smoked oysters. Kojima pointed at each of the items on the menu as he ordered them. Then Maeda carefully poured us each a glass of red wine from a bottle she had just meticulously uncorked.

Cheers, Kojima said, and in return I said, Cheers to you. Sensei flashed through my mind for an instant but I immediately chased his image away. Our glasses clinked. The wine had just the right heft and a subtle dusky aroma.

"That's a nice wine," I said.

Kojima turned to Maeda and said, "So she says."

Maeda gave a slight bow of her head. "I'm just pleased you like it."

Flustered, I bowed my head as well, and Kojima and Maeda both laughed.

"Really, Omachi, you haven't changed a bit," Kojima said, swirling the wine around in his glass and then tasting it. Maeda opened a silver refrigerator that had been built in under the counter and began to prepare the items that Kojima had ordered. I thought about asking about Ayuko—what she was doing these days, what kind of work she did—but since I didn't really care to know, I decided against it. Kojima was still swirling his wine around.

"You know, lots of people do this—swirl their wine around—but I always feel kind of embarrassed when I see them do it." I had been staring fixedly at his fingers as they swirled, and Kojima had followed my gaze from his hands to my face.

"Uh, no, that's not what I was thinking," I stammered, but in fact, I sort of was.

"Just humor me and try it yourself," Kojima urged, looking me deep in the eyes.

"Really?" I said, swirling around the wine in my own glass. The aroma rose to my nostrils. I took a sip, and the wine tasted just the slightest bit different from before. As if there were no resistance. The flavor nestled right up, was perhaps a better way of putting it.

"What a difference," I said, my eyes widening.

Kojima nodded vigorously. "See what I mean?"

"It's amazing."

I felt like I had entered into a strange time, sitting there next to Kojima, in a bar I'd never been to before, swirling wine around in my glass and savoring smoked oysters. Every so often, the thought of Sensei would flit across my mind, but each time, just as suddenly, it would then disappear. It wasn't as though I had returned to my high school days, but neither did it feel like I was actually in the present—all I could say was that I had caught a fleeting moment at the counter of Bar Maeda. It seemed like we had ended up within a time that didn't exist anywhere. The cheese omelet was warm and fluffy. The green salad was peppery. After we worked our way through the bottle of wine, Kojima ordered a vodka cocktail while I ordered a gin cocktail, and we were then surprised by how late it had become. I would have thought it had only just gotten dark out, but it was already past ten o'clock.

"Shall we go?" Kojima, who had grown somewhat taciturn, asked.

"Yes, let's," I answered without thinking. Kojima had only barely mentioned the details of his breakup with Ayuko, and I couldn't really remember what he had said. The ambience in the bar was no longer the crackling mood when they've just opened—by now the air was charged with a dense festivity. At some point, another bartender—a young man—had also appeared behind the counter, and the bar was humming with just the right level of activity. Kojima had apparently taken care of our bill without my noticing. I'll pay my half, I said softly, but Kojima just shook his head gently, replying affably, "Don't worry about it."

I slipped my arm lightly through Kojima's as we slowly climbed the stairs from the underground to the street level.

THE MOON WAS suspended in the sky.

Looking up, Kojima said, "That's your moon," referring to the first character in my name, *tsuki*, the Japanese word for moon. Sensei would never have said such a thing. Abruptly remembering Sensei, I was startled. While we had been inside the bar, I had felt distant and detached from Sensei. Suddenly, I became aware of the weight of Kojima's arm, lightly resting on the small of my back.

"The moon is so round," I said, casually moving my body away from Kojima.

"Yes, it is," he replied, without trying to bridge the distance between us that I had just created. He just stood there, staring up abstractedly at the moon. He looked older than he had when we were in the bar.

"What's wrong?" I asked.

Kojima looked over at me. "Why do you ask?"

"Are you a little tired?"

"Just getting old," Kojima said.

"No, you're not."

"Yes, I am."

"Are not!" I was being unusually obstinate.

Kojima chuckled and bowed his head toward me. "That was rude of me, seeing as how we're the same age."

"Not at all."

I was thinking about Sensei. He had never once referred to himself as "old." Aside from the fact that he was old enough not to make light of his age, it just wasn't in his nature to talk about it. Standing there on the street right then, I felt very far away from Sensei. I was keenly aware of the distance between us. Not only the difference between our age in years, nor even the expanse between where each of us stood at that moment, but rather the sheer distance that existed between us.

Kojima put his arm around my waist once again. To be sure, he didn't exactly encircle my waist so much as hold his arm against the air around my waist. The gesture was quite subtly adept. Since he wasn't actually touching me, there was nothing for me to shake off. I wondered when he had acquired such a skill.

Held this way, I felt as though Kojima were manipulating me like a doll. Kojima hurried across the street and walked into the darkness, taking me along with him. I could see the school ahead of us. The doors of the gate were shut tightly. The school looked huge at night, lit up by the streetlights. Kojima headed up the path to the embankment anyway, and I went along with him.

The cherry blossom party was over. There was not a soul to be found. Not even a stray cat. When the two of us had slipped away, there had been yakitori skewers and empty saké bottles and packets of smoked squid strewn about, and the partygoers had been serried together as they sat on their mats, but now there was no sign of anything on the embankment. All the trash and empty cans had been completely cleared away, and the ground looked as though it had been swept clean with a bamboo broom. Even the garbage cans on the embankment had been emptied of the refuse from the cherry blossom party. It was as if the party had been nothing more than an illusion or a mirage.

"Everything's . . . gone," I said.

"Not surprisingly," Kojima replied.

"Why not?"

"People who are teachers are much more dutiful about upholding public morality."

A few years ago, Kojima said, he had attended one of these annual cherry blossom parties the teachers held right before the start of the school year. He had stayed until the end that time, and as the party drew to a close, he had witnessed the teachers' full-scale cleanup first-hand. There were those who picked up the paper trash and placed it in plastic bags that they had brought for this purpose. There were those who bundled the empty bottles together and piled them on the back of a truck from a liquor store that pulled up to the school entrance just as the party was ending (which, no doubt, Kojima added, had been previously requested to arrive at the given hour). There was the one who distributed any leftover liquor equitably among the teachers who liked to drink. There were those who used brooms from the schoolyard to level out the ground. And there were those who went around picking up whatever had been left behind and collected it all in a box. The teachers worked briskly and efficiently, like a well-trained company of soldiers. Every last vestige of the cherry blossom party—in boisterous celebration until the very last moment—was completely eliminated in less than fifteen minutes.

"I was so astonished, all I could do was just stand there watching," Kojima finished saying.

And so this year as well, that must be how the teachers cleaned up every last trace of the party.

Kojima and I walked around a bit along the area where, not an hour ago, the party's attendees had swarmed. The moon shone brightly. The flowers bloomed pale white, lit up by the moonlight. Kojima led me over to a bench in a corner. He still had his arm circled around my waist, with the same delicate touch.

"I guess I'm a little drunk," Kojima said. His cheeks were flushed, about the same shade of red they had been during the cherry blossom party. Aside from the color in his cheeks, though, his demeanor did not in any way suggest that he was drunk.

"It's still cold out," I said for whatever reason, trying to make conversation. How on earth did I find myself in this situation? Where could Sensei have gone off to? After briskly cleaning up the smoked squid wrappers and yakitori skewers and smoothing out the ground, he and Ms. Ishino were probably out together somewhere.

"Are you cold?" Kojima asked, taking off his jacket and putting it on my shoulders.

"That's not what I meant," I said reflexively.

"Then what did you mean?" Kojima asked, smiling. He had seen right through my knee-jerk reaction. I wasn't at all annoyed to be read so easily, though—rather, I felt like a child hiding something whose parent knows right away what is going on.

The two of us just sat there for a little while, leaning up against each other. Kojima's jacket was warm. It carried a faint hint of cologne. Kojima was still smiling. Despite the fact that we were both facing the same direction, I could tell nonetheless that he was smiling.

"What are you smiling at?" I asked, still facing forward.

"You know, Omachi, you're really just like . . ."

"Like what?"

"Like a high school student. Omachi, don't be nervous." Kojima spoke very softly. Then he put his arms firmly around my shoulders and drew me into an embrace. *Really?* I thought to myself. *Kojima's just going to hug me like this? How strange*, my mind said. But my body quickly responded to him.

"It's cold, why don't we go someplace where it's warm," Kojima whispered.

"Really?" I said out loud.

"Huh?" Kojima responded with surprise.

"Are we really moving that fast?"

Without replying to my question, Kojima hurriedly got up from the bench. Then, turning to me as I still sat there, he touched my chin, raising my face upward, and promptly kissed me.

The kiss happened so fast that I failed to deflect it. *Dammit*, I cursed myself. *That was careless of me.* It was careless, but the kiss wasn't unpleasant. Maybe not unpleasant, but I wasn't happy about it. Rather than happy, it made me feel a little lonely.

"Really?" I asked again.

"Yes, really," Kojima answered, now slightly more self-confident.

Yet I found this situation utterly regrettable. Kojima, still standing, moved in for another kiss.

"Please stop it," I said, trying to be as clear as I could.

"No, I won't," Kojima replied, just as clearly.

"Come on, it's not like you're really serious about me."

Kojima shook his head. "I've liked you all this time, Omachi. Didn't I take you out on that date? Even if it didn't go all that well." His expression was earnest.

"So you've liked me all along?" I asked.

He gave a faint laugh. "I guess life is pretty funny that way."

Kojima looked up at the moon for a moment. It was now enveloped by a thin haze.

Sensei, I thought to myself, and my next thought was *Kojima*.

"Thank you for tonight," I said, staring at his jawline.

"Huh?"

"It was a lovely evening."

The area below Kojima's chin was much thicker than it had been when we were in high school. An accumulation of years. But this stoutness was not at all repugnant. In fact, I rather liked it. I tried to think of what Sensei's jawline looked like. Surely, when Sensei had been the age that Kojima and I were now, his neck must have been appropriately thick. However, the ensuing years had conversely whittled away any heft under his chin.

Kojima was looking at me, a bit surprised. The moon shone brightly, luminous even through the haze.

"So it's not going to happen?" Kojima said, with an exaggerated sigh.

"Seems unlikely."

"Aw, man . . . I'm just terrible on dates," he laughed. I laughed with him.

"No, you're not! You taught me how to swirl my wine and all."

"Yeah, I definitely shouldn't do stuff like that."

Kojima's face was lit by the moonlight. I studied it now.

"Am I a good-looking guy?" he asked as he turned to face my gaze.

"Definitely, you're very good-looking," I answered gamely. Kojima pulled me by the hands up to standing.

"But not good-looking enough for it to happen?"

"You know, I'm a high school girl!"

"As if!" Kojima said, pouting. He too looked like a high school student when he made that face. He looked like a teenager who didn't know the first thing about wine tasting.

We held hands and walked along the embankment. Kojima's hand was warm in mine. The moonlight illuminated the cherry blossoms. I wondered where Sensei was at that moment.

"You know, I never really liked Ms. Ishino," I told Kojima as we walked along.

"Really? Like I said before, I had a crush on her."

"But you didn't like Mr. Matsumoto."

"Right, I thought he was stubborn and strict, you know?"

Little by little, we really were regressing to our high school days. The schoolyard looked white, bathed as it was in moonlight. Perhaps if we kept on walking along the embankment, the years would actually roll back in time.

When we got to the edge of the bank, we turned around and walked back until we reached the entrance to the embankment, and then we made another round trip. The whole time, we held each other's hand tightly. We hardly spoke a word; we just kept walking back and forth along the embankment.

"Shall we go home?" I said, when we came back to the entrance for the umpteenth time. Kojima was silent for a moment until he suddenly let go of my hand.

"I guess so," he replied quietly.

We descended from the embankment side by side. It was close to midnight. The moon had climbed high in the sky.

"I thought we might just keep walking until dawn," Kojima murmured. He didn't turn toward me when he spoke; he seemed to be murmuring these words to the sky.

"I know what you mean," I replied. Kojima stared at me now.

We held each other's gaze for a long moment. Then, without a word, we crossed the street. Kojima hailed a taxi as it sped toward us, and put me inside.

"If I see you home, I'll just get more ideas in my head," Kojima said, smiling.

"All right then," I said, at the same time that the taxi driver slammed the automatic door closed and then sped off.

I turned and watched Kojima's figure retreat from the rear window. It got smaller and smaller, and then disappeared.

Maybe it wouldn't be such a bad thing to get ideas in your head, I muttered softly to myself in the backseat of the taxi. But I was well aware of what would be likely to go wrong in the aftermath. Maybe Sensei was by himself at Satoru's place. Perhaps he was eating salted yakitori. Or else he was cozied up with Ms. Ishino, at the *odenya* or somewhere.

Everything felt so far away. Sensei, Kojima, the moon—they were all so distant from me. I stared out the window, watching the streetscape as it rushed by. The taxi hurtled through the nighttime city. Sensei, I forced out a cry. My voice was immediately drowned out by the sound of the car's engine. I could see many cherry trees in bloom as we sped through the streets. The trees, some young and some many years old, were heavy with blossoms in the night air. Sensei, I called out again, but of course no one could hear me. The taxi carried me along, speeding through the city night.

Lucky Chance

TWO DAYS AFTER the cherry blossom party, I saw Sensei at Satoru's place, but I was just paying my bill when he walked in, so all we said was hello and then parted.

The week after the next, our paths crossed at the tobacco shop in front of the station, but this time Sensei seemed to be in a hurry. All we did was nod at each other and then we parted.

And then it was May. The trees along the streets and the copse next to where I lived grew flush with fresh green leaves. There were days when it seemed hot even in short sleeves, and then there were chilly days that made me long to huddle under the *kotatsu*. I visited Satoru's place several times, and I kept assuming I'd run into Sensei, but I never saw him there.

Sometimes from across the counter, Satoru would ask something like "Tsukiko, do you miss having your dates with Sensei?"

And I would reply, "We never had any dates."

"Is that so?" Satoru would sniff.

I could do without his sniffing. I picked at my flying fish sashimi indifferently. Satoru watched with a criticizing eye as I decimated it. Too bad for the flying fish. But it wasn't my fault. Satoru shouldn't have been the one to go sniffing, "Is that so?"

I continued mistreating the fish. Satoru went back to his cutting board to prepare another customer's order. The flying fish's head shone on the plate. Its wide-open eyes were limpid. With a cry of resolve, I seized a piece of the fish with my chopsticks and dunked it in gingered soy sauce. The firm flesh had a slightly peculiar flavor. I sipped from my glass of cold saké and looked around the bar. Today's menu was written in chalk on the blackboard. MINCED BONITO. FLYING FISH. NEW POTATOES. BROAD BEANS. BOILED PORK. If Sensei were here, he would definitely order the bonito and the broad beans first.

"Speaking of Sensei, the last time I saw him here he was with a beautiful lady," the fat guy in the seat next to me said to Satoru. Satoru barely looked up from his chopping block and, without replying to the guy, he shouted to the interior of the bar, "Bring me one of the blue platters!" A young man appeared from where the back sink was.

"Hey," the fat guy said.

"He's the newbie," Satoru said by way of introduction.

The young man bowed his head and said, "Nice to meet you."

"He looks a bit like you, boss," the guy said.

Satoru nodded. "He's my nephew," he said, and the young man bowed his head once again.

Satoru heaped sashimi onto the platter that the young man had brought from the back. The fat guy stared for a moment at the retreating figure of Satoru's nephew, but soon turned his full attention to his bar snacks.

SHORTLY AFTER THE fat guy left, the other patrons settled up too and the bar was suddenly empty. I could hear the sound of the young man running water in the back. Satoru took a small container from the refrigerator and placed what was inside on two small plates. He set one of the plates in front of me.

"My wife made this recipe, if you care to try it," Satoru said, scooping up some of the other plateful of "his wife's recipe" with his fingers and tossing it in his mouth. The "recipe" was *konnyaku*, which had been stewed with a stronger flavor than the way Satoru made it. This *konnyaku* was piquant with red pepper.

It's good, I said to Satoru, who gave me a serious look and nodded, then scooped up another mouthful. Satoru flipped on the radio that he kept atop a shelf. The baseball game was over and the news was about to start. Advertisements blared one after another for cars and department stores and instant rice with green tea.

"So has Sensei been in here much lately?" I asked Satoru, trying to be as lackadaisical as I could.

"Well, you know," Satoru nodded vaguely.

"That guy who was in here before, he said Sensei'd been here with a beautiful lady." This time I was going for the pleasant, bantering gossip of a regular customer. I'm not actually sure how successful I was, though.

"Um, let's see, I don't really remember," Satoru replied, keeping his head down.

Hmm, I murmured. Hmm, I see.

Both Satoru and I fell silent. On the radio, a reporter was expounding on a theory about a random serial killing spree in another prefecture.

"What kind of person . . . ?" Satoru said.

"What is the world coming to?" I answered.

Satoru listened carefully to the rest of the report and then said, "People have been wondering the same thing for over a thousand years."

Laughter from the young man in the back rang out softly. We could hear him chuckling for a moment but we couldn't tell if he was laughing at what Satoru had said or at something completely unrelated. Could I please have my bill, I said, and Satoru tallied it up in pencil on a piece of paper. Satoru thanked me as I parted the curtain and headed outside, where the nighttime breeze braced against my cheeks. I shivered as I flung the door closed behind me. The wind carried a dampness that smelled like rain. A drop fell on my head. I quickened my pace and headed home.

It rained for the next several days. The color of the young leaves on the trees suddenly intensified—when I looked out the window, everything was green. There was a cluster of still-young zelkova trees growing in front of my apartment. Their green leaves shone glossy and lustrous, battered by the rain. I got a phone call from Takashi Kojima on Tuesday.

"Do you want to go to the movies?" Kojima asked.

Sure, I replied, and I heard him sigh on the other end of the line.

"What's the matter?"

"I'm just nervous. I feel like I'm back in school," Kojima said. "The first time I asked a girl on a date, well, I actually wrote out something like a flow chart of how the conversation might go."

Did you make a flow chart today? I asked.

Kojima answered, "Oh, no," in a serious tone. "But I will admit that I thought about it."

We made plans to meet on Sunday in Yurakucho. Kojima seemed like a classic type. After the movie, we could get something to eat, he had said. By which he undoubtedly meant a fancy Western-style restaurant in Ginza. One of those great places that have been there forever and serve things like tongue stew or cream croquettes.

I thought I might get my hair cut before seeing Kojima, so I went out on Saturday afternoon. Perhaps because of the rain, there weren't as many people out as usual. I walked through the shopping district, twirling my umbrella. How many years had it been that I'd lived in this neighborhood? After I left home, I lived in another part of the city but, like a salmon that returns to the stream of its birth, at some point I ended up back here, in the neighborhood where I grew up.

"Tsukiko." I turned around when I heard my name and saw Sensei standing there. He had on black rain boots and was wearing a raincoat with the belt fastened neatly.

"It's been a long time," he said.

Yes, I replied. It's been a long time.

"You left early, that time at the cherry blossom party."

Yes, I said once more. But I came back again, I added in a quiet voice.

"After the party, I brought Ms. Ishino to Satoru's bar."

He seemed not to have heard me say that I had come back again. Oh? You brought her there? Isn't that nice, I replied dispiritedly. Why was it that when I talked to Sensei I suddenly felt depressed and indignant and strangely sentimental? And I had never been one to wear my emotions on my sleeve.

"Ms. Ishino is quite a genial person, you know. Even Satoru warmed right up to her."

Well, that's Satoru's job, to be nice to the customers, isn't it? But I swallowed my words. Wouldn't this seem to suggest that I was, in fact, feeling jealous toward Ms. Ishino? But that was not the case. I'd be damned if it was.

Sensei held his umbrella completely upright and started walking. I could sense from his gait the tacit but full expectation that I would follow after him. However, I did not, and stood rooted to the spot instead. Sensei walked a ways by himself without turning around.

"Well?" At last realizing he was alone, he turned in my direction and called out leisurely.

"Tsukiko, what's the matter?"

No matter. I'm on my way to the hairdresser's. I have a date tomorrow, I said, unable to help myself.

"A date? With a man?" Sensei asked with interest.

"That's right."

"Really?"

Sensei came back to where I was standing. He peered at me closely in the face.

"What sort of man is he, this man you're going out with?"

"Does it really make a difference?"

"Yes, in fact, it does."

Sensei held his umbrella at a slant. Drops of water trickled down the ribs along the top of the umbrella. Sensei's shoulders got a little wet.

"Tsukiko," Sensei called my name in an extremely serious voice, still staring at me.

"Wh-What is it?"

"Tsukiko," Sensei repeated.

"Yes?"

"Let us go to the pachinko parlor." Sensei's tone was even more grave.

Now? I asked. Sensei nodded solemnly. *Do let's go, right this moment. If we do not go to the pachinko parlor, the world will surely fall apart*, he seemed to suggest.

Yes, I replied, disconcerted. Yes. Do let's, uh, go to the pachinko parlor, then. I followed after Sensei as he went down a side street off the main shopping district.

Inside the pachinko parlor, a traditional battleship march was playing. It was, however, a rather modern rendition. A bass guitar played over the soft sound of wind instruments. Sensei threaded his way between the rows of pachinko machines like he knew just where he was going. He stopped and stood in front of one machine, scrutinizing it carefully, and then moved on to the one next to it. The parlor was crowded. But I imagined it was just as crowded on rainy days as it was on windy days and on sunny days.

"Tsukiko, please choose a machine to your liking." Sensei seemed to have decided upon which machine he was going to sit at. He took out his wallet from the pocket of his raincoat and withdrew a card. Slipping the card noiselessly into a contraption on the side of the machine, he got ¥1,000 worth of balls, and when the card was ejected, he put it away in his wallet.

"Do you come here often?" I asked. Sensei nodded, without saying a word. He seemed completely focused. Sensei carefully manipulated the handle. One ball was launched, and then more balls followed, one after another.

The first ball went in one of the slots. A number of balls flowed out into a dish. Sensei gripped the handle even more assiduously. Several of the balls went into one of the holes along the side of the board, and each time more balls would sputter into the dish.

"You've won so many, Sensei," I called out from behind him, but he just shook his head, not taking his gaze off the board.

"Not quite yet." The moment he said the words, a ball went into a hole at the center of the board and the three symbols in the middle started spinning around. The symbols on the board spun on their own. Keeping his spine completely straight, Sensei calmly continued launching balls, although now it seemed more difficult than before to get the balls to go into the openings.

"They're not going in, are they?" I said, and Sensei nodded.

"I get nervous once this thing starts up," he said.

Two of the symbols matched up. The third and last symbol was still spinning precariously. Just when it seemed like it was about to stop, it would suddenly start spinning wildly again.

"Does something good happen if all three match up?" I asked.

This time, Sensei looked back at me and asked, "Tsukiko, have you never played pachinko before?"

No, never. When I was in elementary school, my dad took me along, so I have played on those old-time machines where you flick each ball. I used to be pretty good at those, actually.

The moment I finished speaking, the third symbol stopped spinning. This last one matched up with the first two.

"Customer number 132 has just won a 'Lucky Chance'! Congratulations!" An announcement came over the loud speaker, and Sensei's machine began flashing wildly.

Without a second glance my way, Sensei remained completely focused on his machine. Quite out of character, his posture was now somewhat rounded. He launched the balls in rapid succession, and they were swallowed up by a large blooming tulip in the center. When that happened, the dish underneath the machine began to overflow with the clinking of pachinko balls. A parlor employee brought over a large square receptacle. Sensei opened the lever at the bottom with his left hand while still gripping the handle with his right hand. The containers were deftly switched, with attention being paid not to allow any more balls to fall into the tulip.

The larger square receptacle was soon full of balls.

"I guess that'll be all," Sensei murmured. When the container was filled just to the brim, the tulip closed and the machine suddenly fell silent. Sensei straightened his back once again and released his grip on the handle.

"So many of them!" I said, and Sensei nodded, still facing forward. He heaved a great sigh.

"Tsukiko, would you like to try?" Sensei turned around to ask. "It will be like sociological research."

Sociological research, indeed. That was so utterly Sensei. I sat down at the machine next to Sensei's. Now, buy some balls for yourself, Sensei advised, so first I bought a card and then tentatively inserted it in the machine to get ¥500 worth.

Following Sensei's example, I sat up straight and tried my best at launching the balls, but none went in. Five hundred yen worth of balls were gone in no time. I took out my card again and bought more balls. This time I tried maneuvering the handle at various angles. Next to me,

Sensei kept calmly launching balls. The symbols in the center remained still, yet a steady stream of balls going in the holes made them emit jingling sounds. The next ¥500 worth also gone, I stopped playing. The symbols on Sensei's machine had started spinning again.

"Will they match up again?" I asked, but Sensei shook his head.

"Most surely not. The odds must be one in a thousand, or more."

Just as he predicted, the symbols lined up haphazardly. Checking to see that the trickle of balls flowing out while he played was now about even with the number of balls that he was using, Sensei stood up. Picking up the full container without effort, he headed toward the counter. After the number of balls was counted for him, Sensei walked around the corner that was decorated with prizes.

"You're not exchanging them for money?" I asked, and Sensei stared at me.

"Tsukiko, you seem to know a lot for someone who doesn't play pachinko."

Yes, well, it's all vicarious, I replied. Sensei laughed. Nevertheless, I would have said that pachinko prizes meant chocolate, but in fact, there were all sorts of things available, from electric rice cookers to neckties. Sensei intently examined each prize. He finally settled on a desktop vacuum in a cardboard box from behind the counter. He exchanged his remaining winnings for chocolate.

HERE, TAKE THE chocolate. Out in front of the parlor, Sensei held out the dozen or so chocolate bars to me.

Sensei, you keep some. I fanned out the bars like a hand of cards when playing old maid, and Sensei took three. Did you play pachinko with Ms. Ishino as well? I asked, nonchalant.

What? Sensei said, tilting his head. Tsukiko, weren't you the one who went off with some young man? he retorted.

What? This time it was I who tilted my head.

Well done, Sensei. You're very good at pachinko, I said.

Sensei made a sour face. One mustn't gamble—it's no good—but I do enjoy pachinko. As he said the words, he carefully adjusted the box with the desktop vacuum cleaner under his arm.

Walking side by side, Sensei and I returned to the shopping district.

Why don't we get a quick drink at Satoru's?

That sounds good.

Don't you have a date tomorrow?

That's all right.

Are you sure?

Yes, I'm sure. We mumbled between ourselves.

It's all right, I repeated to myself as I sidled up to Sensei.

The young leaves had grown into a thick verdure. Sensei and I walked slowly under a single umbrella. Occasionally, Sensei's arm would touch my shoulder. Sensei held the umbrella straight up high.

"I wonder if Satoru's place is open yet," I mused.

Sensei replied, "If not, we can just walk a bit."

"Yes, let's walk then," I said, looking up at Sensei's umbrella.

"Onward, then," Sensei said, echoing the decisiveness of the march that had been playing inside the pachinko parlor.

The rain had softened to a drizzle. A raindrop fell on my cheek. I wiped it away with the back of my hand as Sensei looked on disapprovingly.

"Tsukiko, don't you have a handkerchief?"

"I do, but it's too much trouble to get out."

"Young ladies these days . . ."

I lengthened my gait to match Sensei's robust stride. The sky was brightening and birds had started chirping. The rain was letting up, but Sensei still gripped his umbrella tightly. As he held it aloft, the two of us kept a steady pace, walking along the shopping district.

Spring Thunder

....

TAKASHI KOJIMA INVITED me to go on a trip with him.

"I know an inn that serves the most amazing food," he said.

"Amazing food?" I parroted, and Kojima nodded. His expression was like an earnest schoolchild's. When he was young, he must have looked quite adorable with a *botchan* haircut, I mused.

"Right about now, the *ayu* fish is probably in season."

Hmmm, I replied. A classy inn with delicious cooking. That seemed like just the kind of thing Kojima would suggest.

"What about going to check it out, before the rainy season starts?"

Being with Kojima always brought to mind the word "grown-up."

What I mean is, when Kojima was in elementary school, he was a child, of course. A suntanned kid with thin little shins. In high school, Kojima had seemed like a sprouting boy, on the verge of casting off his boyhood skin and becoming a young man. By the time he got to college, he must have been a full-fledged young man, the epitome of youth. I can just imagine. Now, having reached his thirties, Kojima was a grown-up. No doubt about it.

His behavior was commensurate with his age. The passage of time had been evenly distributed for Kojima, and both his body and mind had developed proportionately.

I, on the other hand, still might not be considered a proper grown-up. I had been very much the adult when I was in elementary school. But as I continued on through junior high and high school, on the contrary, I became less grown-up. And then as the years passed, I turned into quite a childlike person. I suppose I just wasn't able to ally myself with time.

"What happens after the rainy season starts?" I asked.

"Well, we'd get wet," Kojima replied succinctly.

"Not if we used umbrellas," I said, and he laughed.

"Listen, I'm asking you to go on a trip with me, just the two of us. Did you get that?" Kojima peered into my face as he spoke.

"*Ayu* fish, huh?" I was well aware of the fact that Kojima was inviting me on a trip. I also knew that it wouldn't be such a bad thing to go away with him. But then why was I trying to dodge the question?

"They catch the *ayu* in a nearby river. And the local vegetables are also great," Kojima said leisurely. Even though he knew I was hedging, he didn't seem at all concerned; rather, his manner was calm and unhurried.

Kojima went on with his explanation: "Just-picked cucumbers, lightly chopped and dressed with pickled plums. Fresh eggplant, thinly sliced, sautéed, and then drizzled with gingered soy sauce. Cabbage pickled in rice-bran paste. Everything is just like home-cooked food, but the freshness of the vegetables really comes through."

"They're grown and harvested in a field nearby, and prepared within the same day. The miso and soy sauce, they happen to come from a local storehouse too. I think a gourmand like you, Omachi, would really appreciate it," Kojima laughed.

I liked the sound of Kojima's laughter. I was on the verge of saying, Why not, let's go, but then I didn't. *Ayu* fish, huh. Fresh vegetables, I muttered instead, noncommittally.

"Let me know if you decide you want to go. Then I can make a quick reservation," he said casually as he ordered another round.

We were sitting at the counter at Bar Maeda. This was maybe the fifth time Kojima and I had gotten together like this. A small plate was piled with sunflower seeds, and Kojima was munching away. I had snatched a few seeds myself and crunched on them too. Maeda quietly set a Four Roses bourbon and soda in front of Kojima.

Whenever Kojima and I came to Bar Maeda, I always had the feeling that I didn't belong in a place like this. With its jazz standards playing low, its counter polished to a high gleam, its spotlessly clean glasses, the faint scent of tobacco smoke, and the perfect hum of activity—everything was flawless. It made me feel ill at ease.

"These sunflower seeds are good," I said, taking a couple more. Kojima was drinking his bourbon and soda at a leisurely pace. I took a small sip from the glass in front of me. A flawless martini.

I set down my drink with a sigh. The glass was cold, its surface ever so slightly frosted over.

"The rainy season is almost here," Sensei said.

Right, Satoru replied. His nephew nodded too. The young guy was now a regular fixture at the bar.

Sensei turned toward him now to place his order, "*Ayu* fish." The young man replied, "Yessir," and withdrew to the back. The aroma of broiling fish soon wafted out.

"Sensei, do you like *ayu*?" I asked.

"I enjoy most fish, in general. Both saltwater fish and freshwater fish," Sensei answered.

"Really? What about *ayu* fish, then?"

Sensei looked me in the face. Tsukiko, what is it with you and *ayu*? he asked, still staring at me.

Nothing in particular, I hastily replied, looking down. Sensei kept his eye on me for a bit longer, his head tilted to the side.

The young guy came out from the back carrying a plate with the *ayu*. It was served with a sour knotweed sauce.

"The green of the knotweed complements the fresh air during the rainy season," Sensei murmured as he gazed at the fish.

Satoru laughed and said, Sensei, how poetic!

Sensei replied, It's not poetic, it's simply my impression. Using his chopsticks, he carefully broke the *ayu* fish into pieces and began to eat. Sensei's manner of eating was always impeccable.

"Sensei, since you like *ayu* so much, why not go to a hot-spring hotel or someplace to eat it?" I asked.

Sensei raised his eyebrows. "I don't need to go anywhere specifically to eat it," he replied, lowering his eyebrows to their normal position. "What's the matter, Tsukiko? You seem rather peculiar today, indeed."

Takashi Kojima invited me on a trip, I almost blurted out. But of course I didn't. Sensei was drinking his saké at a perfectly reasonable pace. Drinking and then pausing for a spell. He would take another sip, then pause again. I, on the other hand, was draining my cup faster than usual. Pouring and drinking, drinking then pouring. I was already on my third bottle of saké.

"Tsukiko, has something happened?" Sensei asked.

Reflexively I shook my head. Nothing has happened. Nothing, I said. There's no reason to think something has happened, is there?

"If nothing has happened, then there should be no need to deny it so vehemently." The *ayu* fish was already no more than just bones. Sensei nudged the delicate skeleton with his chopsticks. It had been picked perfectly clean. The *ayu* was delicious, Sensei said to Satoru.

Thanks, Satoru replied. I hurried to drain my cup. Sensei looked at the empty cup in my hand with a reproachful expression.

You've had enough for tonight, Tsukiko, he said gently.

Please leave me alone, I replied, filling my cup with saké. I drank that down in one gulp, having now emptied my third bottle.

"One more!" I ordered another from Satoru. Saké, he shouted curtly toward the back.

Tsukiko, Sensei said as he peered at me, but I turned my face away. "Well, you can't take your order back now, but you mustn't drink the whole thing," he said in an unusually stern tone. As he spoke the words, he tapped me on the shoulder.

Yes, I replied quietly. The alcohol had suddenly hit me. Sensei, could you please tap me again? I said, the words a jumble in my mouth.

Tsukiko, you are like a spoiled child tonight, he laughed, lightly tapping my shoulder several times.

That's because I am a spoiled child. Always have been, I said, reaching out to touch the *ayu* bones on Sensei's plate. The soft bones were pliant. Sensei removed his hand from my shoulder and slowly brought his cup to his lips. For a moment I leaned up against Sensei. Then I quickly moved away. Whether or not Sensei noticed me leaning against him, he kept his cup at his mouth and said not a word.

WHEN I CAME TO, I was in Sensei's house.

I seemed to be lying directly on the floor in the tatami room. Above my head was the low dining table, and right in front of me I could see Sensei's legs. "Oh," I said as I sat up.

"You're awake?" Sensei said. The rain shutters as well as the doors were open. The night air was streaming into the room. It was a little cold. I could faintly make out the moon in the sky, swathed in a thick halo.

"Was I sleeping?" I asked.

"You were sleeping," Sensei laughed. "You had quite a good rest there."

I looked at the clock. It was just past twelve midnight.

"I didn't sleep that much, did I? It was about an hour."

"To sleep for an hour at someone else's house is plenty," Sensei laughed anew. His face was redder than usual. I wondered if he had been drinking the whole time I was asleep.

What am I doing here? I asked.

Sensei opened his eyes wide. You don't remember? The way you carried on, I want to go to your house, I want to go!?

Did I really? I said, lying back down on the tatami. I could feel the straw weave on my cheek. My tangled hair fanned out over the mat. I lay there, watching the night clouds roll by. I didn't want to go on a trip with Kojima. The thought came clearly to mind. With the distinct feeling of the tatami weave on my cheek, I thought about the vague sense of discomfort I experienced when I was with Kojima—it was faint yet inconsolable.

"I'll have tatami marks here," I said, still sprawled on the floor.

"Where?" Sensei asked. He had come around the table to my side.

"Ah, I see. You're really laid up against it, aren't you?" Sensei said, lightly touching my cheek. His fingers were cold. Sensei seemed bigger to me. Probably because I was looking up at him from below.

"Your cheek is warm, Tsukiko."

He was still touching my cheek. The clouds were moving fast. At times the moon would be completely hidden behind the clouds, then the next moment part of it would appear again.

I'm drunk, that's why I'm hot, I replied. Sensei was trembling slightly. I wondered if he was drunk too.

"Sensei, what if we went somewhere together?" I asked.

"Where would we go?"

"Maybe a delicious inn where they have *ayu* fish?"

"I can get all the *ayu* I need at Satoru's place." Sensei pulled his fingers away from my cheek.

"Then what about a remote mountainside hot-spring spa?"

"There's no need to go all the way into the mountains when the public bath around the corner is just fine." Sensei was next to me, sitting on his heels with his legs folded under him. He was no longer trembling. His posture was perfectly straight, as always.

I sat up. "Let's go somewhere, just the two of us," I said, looking Sensei in the eye.

"I'm not going anywhere," he replied, staring straight back at me.

"No! I want us to go!"

I must have been drunk. I myself could only half-understand what I was babbling on about. Although the truth was that I fully understood, my head seemed to be pretending I was only half-aware of my own words.

"Tsukiko, where on earth would we go?"

"We could go anywhere at all, as long as I'm with you," I cried.

The night clouds were moving fast. The wind had picked up strength. The air was heavy with humidity.

"You'd better settle down, Tsukiko," Sensei said lightly.

"I'm settled down enough."

"It's time to go home, you should go to bed."

"I will not go home."

"Don't you think you're being unreasonable?"

"I'm not the least bit unreasonable! What I mean is, Sensei, I love you!"

The moment I said this, my belly blazed with warmth.

I had screwed up. Grown-ups didn't go around blurting out troublesome things to people. You couldn't just blithely disclose something that would then make it impossible to greet them with a smile the next day.

But I had gone and said it. Because I wasn't a grown-up. I never would be, not like Kojima. Sensei, I love you, I repeated one more time, as if to be doubly sure. Sensei just stared at me with astonishment.

· · ·

THUNDER RUMBLED OFF in the distance. After a little while, there was a flash of light among the clouds. It must have been lightning. A few seconds later, thunder could be heard again.

"This strange weather must be a result of the strange thing you said, Tsukiko," Sensei murmured, leaning forward from the veranda.

It wasn't strange, I retorted. Sensei gave a wry smile.

"It looks like we'll have a bit of a storm." Sensei put up the rain shutters with a loud clatter. They didn't slide very well. He also closed the doors. The lightning was flashing wildly, and the thunder was growing near.

Sensei, I'm scared, I said, going to his side.

"There's nothing to be scared of. It's merely an electrical discharge phenomenon," Sensei replied quite calmly while trying to avoid my encroachment. I scooted closer to him.

The truth is, I'm very frightened of thunder. I'm not trying to make something happen between us, really, this is just about being scared, I said through clenched teeth. The thunderstorm was already quite intense, lightning flashes followed the next moment by rumbling thunder. And it had started to rain—the sound of it driving against the rain shutters was loud.

"Tsukiko?" Sensei peered at me. I was sitting beside him, stiff as a board, with both hands over my ears.

"You really are terrified, aren't you?"

I nodded silently. Sensei stared at me solemnly, and then he began to laugh.

"My dear, you are a strange young lady," he said, laughing gleefully.

Come over here, let me hold you. Sensei drew me close. He smelled like alcohol. The sweet smell of saké wafted from Sensei's chest. Still sitting on his heels, he laid my torso across his knees and embraced me tightly.

Sensei, I said, in a voice that sounded like a sigh.

Tsukiko, he replied. His voice was extremely clear; he sounded very much like himself. Children think the strangest things, don't they? Because anyone who is afraid of thunder is nothing more than a child.

Sensei laughed loudly. His laughter reverberated with the rumbling thunder.

Sensei, I meant it when I said I love you. I spoke these words as I lay atop Sensei's knees, but he didn't hear me at all—my words were lost amid the thunder and Sensei's booming laughter.

The thunderstorm grew more and more intense. The rain beat down in torrents. Sensei was laughing. And here I was, bewildered, lying across Sensei's knees. What would Kojima say, if he could see us now?

It was all somehow absurd. Me declaring my love for Sensei to his face, Sensei taking it rather completely in stride yet without responding to my declaration, the sudden outbreak of the thunderstorm, the increasingly oppressive humidity in the room now that the rain shutters were closed—everything seemed like it was part of a dream.

Sensei, am I dreaming? I asked.

It sure seems like it, doesn't it? he replied merrily.

If this is a dream, when will I wake up?

Hmm, I can't say.

I wish I didn't have to wake up.

But if this is a dream, then we must wake up sometime.

A huge crack of resounding thunder immediately followed a bolt of lightning, and my body stiffened. Sensei rubbed my back.

I don't want to wake up, I said again.

That's fine, Sensei replied.

The rain beat down hard on the roof. I kept my body rigid atop Sensei's knees as Sensei calmly rubbed my back.

The Island, Part 1

AND SO IT was that, after all, I found myself here.

Sensei's briefcase sat in a corner of the room. The same briefcase he always carried.

"All of your things fit into that briefcase?" I had asked him while we were en route on the train. Sensei nodded.

"This briefcase is more than big enough for two days' change of clothes."

I see, I said. Sensei's hands lightly held the briefcase on his knees as he gave himself over to the rocking of the train. Both Sensei and the briefcase swayed back and forth in short, quick motions.

We rode the train together, we took the ferry together, we climbed the hill on the island together, and we came to this small guesthouse together.

Had Sensei given in and decided to go on a trip because of all my pleading that night—the night of the thunderstorm that heralded the rainy season? Or had he made up his mind about it, had a sudden change of heart, sometime after the storm had passed, while he lay quietly in the room next to where I too lay quietly alone on the extra bedding that Sensei had carefully spread out for me? Or was it that,

for no particular reason and without any motivation, Sensei was seized
with an urge to travel all of a sudden?

"Tsukiko, would you like to go to an island with me next Saturday and Sunday?" Sensei had said out of the blue. We were on our way
home from Satoru's place. The street was wet from the ongoing rain.
Several puddles of water caught the reflection of the streetlights and
they seemed to glow white in the night. Sensei didn't bother trying to
avoid walking in the puddles; he just kept going steadily ahead. I tried
to sidestep them one by one, and so I weaved randomly this way and
that, as opposed to Sensei's swift progress.

"Huh?" I responded.

"Didn't you suggest that we go on an excursion the other night?"

"An excursion?" I repeated Sensei's words like an idiot.

"There's an island that I've visited from time to time in the past."

Sensei mentioned that he had often traveled to this island. For
some kind of reason, he muttered.

What was the reason? I asked, but Sensei did not reply. Instead he
quickened his step.

"If you're busy, Tsukiko, I will go on my own."

"I'll go, I'll go," I replied hurriedly.

And so it was that here I found myself.

On the island where Sensei had traveled "for some kind of reason." At a small guesthouse. Sensei carried his same briefcase, and I
carried a brand-new suitcase I had bought for the occasion. The two
of us. Together. To be sure, we had separate rooms. Sensei had strongly
suggested that I take a room with a view of the sea, while he took a
room facing the island's interior hillside.

No sooner had I deposited my luggage in the alcove of my sea-
side room than I was knocking on Sensei's door. Knock-knock. It's
your mother. Open the door, dear little goats. I am not the wolf. Look
how white my paw is.

Sensei simply opened the door, without bothering to look at my
paw first.

"Would you like some tea?" Sensei grinned as he invited me in. I grinned back.

Sensei's room seemed slightly smaller than mine, even though it was the same six-mat size. Perhaps because the window looked out on the mountain.

"Why don't we go to my room? The view of the sea is lovely," I said, but Sensei shook his head.

"A man mustn't barge into a lady's room."

I see, I replied. You may barge in, if you like, I was about to add, but I didn't think that Sensei would find that amusing, so I stopped myself.

I could not imagine what Sensei had in mind when he invited me on this trip. His face had betrayed nothing when I agreed to go along with him, and on the train he had been exactly the same Sensei as always. Even here, now, sipping tea, his manner was no different from at Satoru's place when the counter was full and we ended up sitting across from each other at a small table.

Yet still, here we were, the two of us.

"Would you like another cup of tea?" I asked cheerfully.

"I would indeed, please," Sensei replied. Even more jauntily, I refilled the teapot with hot water. I could hear seagulls crying out from the mountainside. The seagulls' calls sounded rambunctious and rowdy. They seemed to be flying back and forth and all around the island during this hour of evening calm.

"WE'LL MAKE A round," Sensei said as he stood in the guesthouse's foyer putting on his shoes. When I went to put on a pair of sandals that had the name of the guesthouse written in marker, Sensei paused.

"This island is surprisingly hilly, with rough terrain," he said, pointing to my shoes that were placed neatly in the shoe cupboard. They had just the slightest heel. When I wore them, the top of my head reached Sensei's eyes.

"But my shoes aren't fit for walking hills," I replied, and Sensei frowned faintly. So faintly that no one else would have noticed. However, now even the subtlest changes in Sensei's facial expressions did not escape me.

"Sensei, please don't make that face."

"What face?"

"Like you've seen something that bothers you."

"There's nothing in particular bothering me, Tsukiko."

"Something's bothering you."

"That's not the case."

"No, no matter what anyone else says, I think there's something bothering you!"

It had devolved into a silly argument. I slipped on a pair of the guesthouse sandals and followed after Sensei. Empty-handed, Sensei wore a vest, his posture stick-straight as he walked along slowly.

The evening calm had passed and a light breeze had begun to blow. There were cumulonimbus clouds along the horizon on the beach. The sun, about to set into the sea, bathed all of the clouds in a pink light.

"How long does it take to circle the island?" I asked, out of breath from the hill. Just like that time we went mushroom hunting with Satoru and Toru, Sensei was not the least bit winded. He climbed the island's steep slopes without any difficulty.

"At a quick pace, about an hour."

"At a quick pace?"

"At Tsukiko's pace, it would probably take about three hours."

"Three hours?"

"You ought to exercise more, Tsukiko."

Sensei just kept steadily walking along. I gave up trying to keep in step with him, stopping midway up the hill to look at the sea. The setting sun was getting closer to the water. The cumulonimbus clouds were deepening to a flaming vermilion. I wondered where we were.

What the hell was I doing here, on a hillside in some strange fishing town, surrounded by the sea? Sensei's figure up ahead of me grew more distant. His back seemed somehow cold and remote. Despite the fact that we had come on this trip together—even if it was only a two-day trip—I felt as if the person moving steadily away from me, Sensei, was a stranger.

"Don't worry, Tsukiko," Sensei turned around to face me.

Huh? I said from down below on the slope. Sensei gave a little wave of his hand.

"It's only a little bit farther from the top of this hill."

Is the island really that small? Climbing this hill puts us all the way around the island? I asked. Sensei waved his hand again.

"Tsukiko, don't be absurd. How could that possibly be?"

"But you said . . ."

"We couldn't make it all the way around with someone as out-of-shape as you along, and wearing those sandals, no less."

He was still stuck on the sandals. Hurry up! Don't just stand there! Sensei hastened me along as I held my head high.

"Where the hell are we going anyway?"

"Stop grumbling now, and come up here."

Sensei had swiftly climbed the slope. The last part of it was even steeper, as it circled around the hill. I could no longer see Sensei. Hastily I slid my feet farther into the sandals and followed after him. Sensei, please wait for me. I'm on my way. I'm coming now, I said as I followed him.

When I reached the top of the slope, I found myself at the summit. It was spacious and wide open. There were tall, dense trees along the path that continued up from the slope. Several houses were nestled among the trees, forming a hamlet. Each home was bordered by small plots in which cucumbers and tomatoes were being grown. Beside the fields were chicken coops, and I could hear the serene sound of clucking from beyond the rough chicken wire.

Past the hamlet, there was a small marsh. Perhaps because it was getting dark around us, the marsh was immersed in a deep green. Sensei was standing alongside, waiting for me.

"Tsukiko, this way." Backlit by the setting sun, his face and figure looked pitch-black. I couldn't see Sensei's expression at all. I walked over by his side, dragging my feet in the sandals.

The marsh was covered with duckweed and water hyacinths and the like. Dozens of water striders were skimming lightly along its surface. Now that I was standing next to Sensei, I could make out his face. His mien was placid, like the surface of the marsh.

"Shall we go on?" Sensei said as he stepped forward. It was a little marsh. The road circled all the way around it, now with a slight descent. Instead of tall trees, it was bordered with more shrubs. The road narrowed, the paving patchy in places.

"We're here." It was now virtually unpaved, just bare ground. Sensei went along the dirt road slowly. I followed him, my sandals making a pitter-patter.

A small cemetery appeared before us.

THE GRAVESTONES NEAR the entrance were tidily maintained but, further inside, the spindle-shaped tombstones and mossy ancient-looking graves were overgrown with weeds. Trampling the knee-high grasses, Sensei proceeded farther into the graveyard.

"Sensei, how far are you going?" I called after him. Sensei turned back and smiled. An extremely kind smile.

"It's not far. Look, here it is," Sensei said, as he crouched before a small gravestone. This one was not quite as moss-covered as the other old graves near it, but still, the small marker was swathed in a damp green. There was a chipped bowl in front of it, about half-full of what must have been rainwater. A horsefly buzzed about, flitting around Sensei's and my head.

Still crouching, Sensei joined his hands in prayer. He closed his eyes, praying earnestly. The horsefly alighted alternately on me and on Sensei. Each time it landed on me, I shooed it away, but Sensei kept on praying, seemingly unbothered.

After a while, Sensei unclasped his joined palms and stood up. He looked at me.

"Is this a relative's grave?" I asked.

"I'm not sure if I would say a relative," Sensei replied ambiguously.

The horsefly landed on top of Sensei's head. This time he seemed to notice, and he swatted at his head. As if surprised, the horsefly flew off in retreat.

"It's my wife's grave."

Huh? I swallowed my surprise. Sensei smiled again. That extremely kind smile.

"She died on this island."

After she ran away from her home with Sensei, she ended up in the village on the mainland where we took the ferry to this island, Sensei explained in a detached tone. She had soon broken up with the man with whom she fled, and there were several others, but Sensei's wife settled down with the last man with whom she lived in the village at the tip of the cape. And when had she come to this island, whose shore looks so close from the village? One day Sensei's wife and her last lover came over, and she was struck by a car, rarely seen on the island, and she died.

"She lived quite a bohemian life," Sensei said with a grave look as he concluded the story about his wife's past.

"Indeed."

"And what's more, a singular life."

"Indeed."

"All that to be hit by a car on this sleepy little island," Sensei said feelingly, and then gave a little laugh. I turned to face the grave, clasped my hands lightly, then looked up at Sensei. He was still smiling as he looked down at me.

"I thought we should come here together, Tsukiko," Sensei said softly.

"Together?"

"Yes, it had been a while since I'd visited."

A flock of seagulls hovered above the cemetery, their cries raising a commotion. I tried to ask, Why would you think to bring me here? But the seagulls were wild with excitement. My words were drowned out by their cries and Sensei didn't hear me.

"I've never understood . . . ," Sensei murmured, gazing up at the seagulls in the sky. "It seems that, even now, I still dwell on my wife."

The words "even now" reached me between the seagulls' cries. Even now. Even now. *Did you bring me all the way to this desolate island just to tell me that?* I screamed in my head. But, of course, I didn't say this either. I stared at Sensei. He wore a soft smile. What the hell was he smiling so blithely about?

"I'm going back to the guesthouse," I said finally, turning my back on Sensei.

Tsukiko, I thought I heard him call out after me, but I might have been imagining it. I followed along the path from the cemetery to the marsh at a trot, passing through the hamlet and down the hill. I kept turning around but Sensei wasn't following me. I thought I heard his voice call out my name again.

Sensei, I called back. The seagulls wouldn't shut up. I waited a moment, but I didn't hear Sensei's voice again. Apparently, he wasn't coming after me. Was he sitting alone in the cemetery, praying? Feelingly? About his wife that he still dwells on? His dead wife?

Old bastard, I said to myself, and then I repeated it out loud. "Old bastard!" *The old bastard must be taking a brisk walk around the island. I should just forget about him and go soak in the little outdoor hot spring at the guesthouse. Since I'm here on this island anyway. I'm going to enjoy myself on this trip whether Sensei is with me or not. I've managed on my*

*own until now anyhow. I drink by myself, I get drunk by myself, and I have
a good time by myself, don't I?*

I made my way down the hill with determination. The setting sun
was still hovering over the water, about to disappear. The loud patter-
ing of my sandals annoyed me. The seagulls' cries that filled the entire
island were relentless. The new dress that I had worn especially for
this trip was uncomfortable around my waist. The too-big sandals had
made my insteps hurt. The road and the beach without a soul to be seen
were lonesome. And Sensei—damn him for not coming after me—had
pissed me off.

This was just what my life was like, after all. Here I was, trudg-
ing alone on an unfamiliar road, on some unfamiliar island, separated
from Sensei—whom I thought I knew but didn't know at all. There
was no reason not to start drinking. I had heard that the island's
specialties were octopus, abalone, and giant prawns. I was going to
eat a shitload of abalone. Sensei had invited me, so it ought to be his
treat. And tomorrow when I'm so hungover I can't walk, he can carry
me on his back. I would totally forget about whatever notions I had
momentarily entertained regarding what it might be like to spend
time with Sensei.

The lights under the guesthouse's eaves were illuminated. Two
large seagulls were perched on the roof. Hunched and still, they looked
like guardian deities on the edge of the roof tiles. It was now completely
dark and, without my noticing it, the seagulls' cries had ceased. As I
rattled open the front door of the guesthouse, I called out, I'm back.
I heard a cheerful voice from inside say, Welcome back! The aroma of
freshly cooked rice wafted toward me. Looking out from inside, it was
pitch-black.

Sensei, it's dark, I murmured. Sensei, come back, it's dark already. I
don't care if you're still dwelling on your wife or whatever, just hurry back
and let's have a drink together. My earlier anger was now completely

forgotten. We don't have to be teatime companions, we can just be drinking buddies. I'd like nothing more than that. Hurry back now, I murmured over and over, out toward the dark night. I thought I saw Sensei's silhouette in the dimness on the hill outside the guesthouse. But there wasn't a silhouette at all, not even a shadow to be seen, only darkness. Sensei, hurry back, I would go on murmuring forever.

The Island, Part 2

"LOOK, TSUKIKO, THE octopus is floating to the top," Sensei pointed out, to which I nodded.

It was sort of like an octopus version of *shabu-shabu*. Thin, almost-transparent slices of octopus were submerged in a gently boiling pot of water, and then immediately plucked out with chopsticks when they rose to the surface. Dipped in *ponzu* sauce, the sweetness of the octopus melted in your mouth with the *ponzu's* citrus aroma, creating a flavor that was quite sublime.

"See how the octopus's translucent flesh turns white when you put it in hot water," Sensei chatted exactly the same way as if he and I were sitting and drinking at Satoru's place.

"It's white, yes." I, on the other hand, was decidedly unsettled. I had no idea whether I ought to smile or be quiet, or how I should behave at all.

"But, just before, there's a moment when it appears ever so slightly pink, don't you see?"

"Yes," I replied quietly. Sensei looked at me with a bemused expression and then helped himself to three slices of octopus at once from the pot.

"You're awfully acquiescent tonight, Tsukiko."

Sensei had finally come down the hill after a really long time. The seagulls' cries had fallen completely silent and the darkness had grown thick and dense. A really long time, I thought, but then again it may not have been more than five minutes. I had stood and waited for him at the guesthouse's front door. He had returned, his footsteps light and not the least bit uncertain in the dark. When I called out to him, "Sensei," he replied, "Ah, Tsukiko, I'm back." As we headed into the guesthouse alongside each other, I said, "Welcome back."

"Such splendid abalone!" Sensei exclaimed as he lowered the flame under the pot of octopus *shabu-shabu*. Four abalone shells were lined up on a medium-sized plate, each shell filled with abalone cut into sashimi.

"Have your fill, Tsukiko."

Adding a little wasabi, Sensei dunked a piece of abalone in soy sauce. He chewed it slowly. His mouth while chewing was the mouth of an old man. I chewed the abalone too. I hoped that my mouth was still that of a young woman, but if not, I was resigned to that too. I felt very strongly about it at that moment.

Octopus *shabu-shabu*. Abalone. *Mirugai*. *Kochi* fish. Boiled *shako*. Fried giant prawns. They were served one after another. By now, the pace of Sensei's chopsticks began to slow. He barely tipped his saké, taking small sips. I inhaled the rapid-fire offerings, drinking cup after cup without saying much of anything.

"Are you enjoying the food, Tsukiko?" Sensei asked, as if he were indulging a grandchild with a voracious appetite.

"It's delicious," I replied brusquely, then I repeated myself, this time with a bit more enthusiasm.

By the time they brought out the cooked and pickled vegetables, both Sensei and I had eaten our fill. We decided not to have any rice, just some miso soup. The two of us finished our saké leisurely as we sipped the soup, rich with fish stock.

"Well, is it about time to go?" Sensei stood up, holding his room key. I followed him to stand, but apparently the saké had had more of an effect than I realized and my feet were unsteady. I stumbled as I took a step, falling forward onto my hands on the tatami.

"Oh, dear," Sensei said, looking down at me.

"Stop with your 'Oh, dear' and give me a hand!" I sort of shouted, and Sensei laughed.

"There, now you sound like Tsukiko!" he said, holding out a hand. I took it and climbed the steps. We stopped outside Sensei's room, which was halfway down the corridor. Sensei put his key in the lock. It made a clicking sound. I stood there, swaying in the hall, as I watched Sensei's back.

"You know, Tsukiko, the hot spring at this guesthouse is supposed to be quite good," Sensei turned around to say.

All right, I replied vacantly, still swaying.

"Once you've had a moment, go take a bath."

All right.

"It will sober you up a bit."

All right.

"Once you've taken the waters, if the night is still long, come to my room."

This time, instead of replying All right again, my eyes widened. Huh?!? What do you mean by that?

"I don't mean anything by that," Sensei answered, disappearing behind the door.

The door closed before me and I was left standing in the corridor, now only slightly swaying. In my saké-addled mind, I ruminated about what Sensei had said. Come to my room. He had definitely said those words. But, if I went to his room, what exactly would happen? Surely we wouldn't just be playing cards. Maybe we'd keep drinking. Then again, it was Sensei—he might suddenly suggest, "Let's write some poetry," or something like that.

"Now, Tsukiko, don't get your hopes up," I muttered, heading for my own room. I unlocked the door and flipped on the light switch, and there in the middle of the room, my single bedding had been laid out. My luggage had been moved in front of the alcove.

As I changed into a *yukata* and got ready for the bath, I repeated over and over, "Don't get your hopes up, don't get your hopes up."

THE HOT SPRING made my skin soft. I washed my hair, immersing myself in the bath over and over, and by the time I had painstakingly blown my hair dry in the changing room, to my surprise, more than an hour had passed.

I went back to my room and opened the window, letting the night air rush in. The crashing of the waves sounded much louder now. I leaned against the window sash for a while.

Since when had Sensei and I become close like this? At first, Sensei had been a distant stranger. An old, unfamiliar man who in the faraway beyond had been a high school teacher of mine. Even once we began chatting now and then, I still barely ever looked at his face. He was just an abstract presence, quietly drinking his saké in the seat next to mine at the counter.

It was only his voice that I remembered from the beginning. He had a resonant voice with a somewhat high timbre, but it was rich with overtones. A voice that emanated from the boundless presence by my side at the counter.

At some point, sitting beside Sensei, I began to notice the heat that radiated from his body. Through his starched shirt, there came a sense of Sensei. A feeling of nostalgia. This sense of Sensei retained the shape of him. It was dignified, yet tender, like Sensei. Even now, I could never quite get a hold on this sense—I would try to capture it, but the sense escaped me. Just when I thought it was gone, though, it would cozy back up to me.

I wondered, for instance, if Sensei and I were to be together, whether that sense would temper into solidity. But then again, wasn't a sensation just that kind of indistinct notion that slips away, no matter how you try to contain it?

A large moth flew into my room, attracted by the light. It flitted about, scattering the scales from its wings. I pulled the cord on the lamp, and the bright white light of the bulb softened to an orange glow. The moth idly fluttered about before finally drifting back outside.

I waited a moment, but the moth did not return.

I closed the window, retied the obi on my *yukata*, applied a little lipstick, and grabbed a handkerchief. I went out into the corridor, trying not to make a sound as I locked the door. Several small moths had gathered around the light in the hallway. Before knocking on Sensei's door, I took a deep breath. I pressed my lips together lightly, smoothed my hair with the palm of my hand, and then took another deep breath.

"Sensei," I called out, and from within I heard the reply, "It's open." I carefully turned the doorknob.

Sensei was resting his elbows on the low table. He was drinking a beer, his back to the bedding that had been moved off to the side.

"Is there no saké?" I asked.

"No, there's some in the refrigerator, but I've had enough already," he said as he tilted a five-hundred-milliliter bottle of beer. The foam rose cleanly in his glass. I took a glass that was upside down on a tray on top of the refrigerator.

Please, I said, holding it out in front of Sensei. He smiled and poured the same clean head of beer for me.

There were a few triangular pieces of cheese wrapped in silver foil on the table.

"Did you bring those with you, Sensei?" I asked, and he nodded.

"You came prepared."

"I thought of it just as I was leaving and threw them in my briefcase."

The night was tranquil. The sound of the waves could be heard through the window. Sensei opened a second bottle of beer. The popping sound of the bottle opener echoed throughout the room.

By the time we finished the second bottle, both of us had fallen silent. Every so often the sound of the waves grew louder.

"It's so quiet," I said, and Sensei nodded.

A little while later, Sensei said, "It's very quiet," and this time I nodded.

The silver foil wrappers from the cheese had been peeled off and lay curled up on the table. I gathered the foil into a ball. I suddenly remembered how, when I was little, I had collected the silver foil from chocolate fingers and had fashioned a rather large ball out of them. I would carefully unfold each piece, flattening them out as best I could. Occasionally, I came across a gold wrapper, and I would set these aside. I had a vague memory of saving these in the bottom drawer of my desk, with the idea to use them as a Christmas tree topper. But then, when Christmas came round, I seem to recall that the gold paper had gotten buried under my notebooks and my modeling clay set, and had been crushed and wrinkled.

"It's so quiet." Who knows how many times it was said, but this time Sensei and I had both said it at the same time. Sensei adjusted his seat on the cushion. I did the same. I sat across from Sensei, playing with the silver foil ball in my hands.

Sensei opened his mouth as if to say, "Oh," but no sound came out. His open mouth showed signs of his age. Much more so than earlier, when he had been chewing the abalone. Softly, I averted my gaze. Sensei did the same.

The sound of the waves was constant.

"Perhaps it's time to go to sleep," Sensei said quietly.

"Yes," I replied. What else was there to say? I stood up and closed the door behind me, and I walked back to my room. There were now even more moths clustered around the light in the hallway.

I AWOKE WITH a start in the middle of the night.

My head hurt a little. There was no sign of anyone else in my room. I tried to revive that indefinite sense of Sensei without much success.

Once I wake up I never get back to sleep. The ticking of my watch by the pillow rang in my ears. Just when I thought it was so close, it would recede. But the watch was always in the same place. How strange.

For a while I just lay still. Then I began to stroke my own breast under my *yukata*. It was neither soft nor hard. I let my hand slip down to caress my belly. My belly felt very smooth. And further on down. My palm brushed against something warm. Despite my idle touch, though, it wasn't the least bit pleasurable. Then I thought about whether I had any hope or expectation about being touched by Sensei, and whether that would be pleasurable, but that seemed futile as well.

I must have lain there for about thirty minutes. I thought I might fall back asleep, just listening to the sound of the waves, but instead I was wide-awake. I wondered what the chances were that Sensei too was lying there, awake in the dark.

Once the thought occurred to me, the idea steadily expanded in my mind. Soon enough, I became convinced that Sensei was calling me from the other room. If not kept in check, nighttime thoughts are prone to amplification. I couldn't lie still any longer. Without turning on the light, I opened the door to my room very quietly. I went to the bathroom at the end of the corridor and used the toilet. I thought that if my bladder could relax, perhaps my exaggerated mood might deflate as well. But my mind still wasn't the least bit eased.

I returned to my room and applied a bit of lipstick, then I tiptoed over to Sensei's room. I put my ear to the door, trying to listen inside. Just like a thief. Rather than the sound of him breathing, I could hear some other kind of sound. I stood there for a moment, listening carefully, and now and then the sound grew louder. Sensei, I whispered. Sensei, what's the matter? Are you all right? Is there something wrong? Should I come in?

SUDDENLY THE DOOR opened. I shut my eyes to the flood of light from within the room.

"Tsukiko, don't just stand there, come inside!" Sensei beckoned to me. Once I had opened my eyes, they adjusted to the light immediately. It appeared that Sensei had been doing some kind of writing. Papers were strewn about the table.

What are you writing? I asked, and Sensei picked up a sheet of paper from the table to show me.

OCTOPUS FLESH, FAINTLY RED was written on the page. I gazed at it for a good long while, and then Sensei said, "I can't seem to come up with the final syllables."

He mused, "What might come after 'faintly red'?"

I flopped down to sit on a cushion. While I had been agonizing over my feelings for Sensei, he had been agonizing over the puzzle of the octopus.

"Sensei," I said in a low voice. Sensei raised his head absently. On one of the sheets strewn on top of the table, there was a lame attempt at a drawing of an octopus. The octopus had a dotted *hachimaki* tied around its head.

"What is it, Tsukiko?"

"Sensei, that . . ."

"Yes?"

"Sensei, this . . ."

"Yes?"

"Sensei."

"Whatever's the matter, Tsukiko?"

"How about 'the roaring sea'?"

I could not seem to bring myself to the heart of the matter. I wasn't even sure if there was such a thing as "the heart of the matter" between Sensei and me.

"Oh, you mean, 'Octopus flesh, faintly red, the roaring sea'?"

Sensei paid no attention to my desperate state at all, or else he pretended not to notice, as he wrote the verse on the page. Octopus flesh, faintly red, the roaring sea, he recited as he wrote.

"That's quite good. Tsukiko, you have a fine aesthetic."

I murmured a vague reply. Furtively, so that Sensei wouldn't see, I brought a piece of scrap paper to my lips and wiped away the lipstick. Sensei muttered to himself as he fine-tuned the haiku.

"Tsukiko, what do you think of 'The roaring sea, octopus flesh, faintly red'?"

There was nothing to think about it. I parted my now colorless lips to murmur another vague response. Having transferred the poem to the page with obvious delight, Sensei now shook his head, somewhat skeptically.

"It's Basho," Sensei said. I didn't have it in me to reply, all I could do was simply nod my head. Basho's poem is "The darkening sea, a wild duck calls, faintly white." As he continued writing, Sensei began to lecture. Here, now, in the middle of the night.

You could say that the haiku we have written together is based on Basho's haiku. It has an interesting broken meter. "The darkening sea, faintly white, a wild duck calls" doesn't work, because this way "faintly white" carries over to both the sea and the duck's call. When it comes at the end, it brings the whole haiku to life. Do you understand? See? Tsukiko, go ahead, write another poem.

So, with no choice, I found myself sitting there with Sensei, writing poetry. How did this come about? It was already past two o'clock in the morning. What was the state of affairs that had me counting out syllables on my fingertips and scribbling out mediocre poetry like "Moths at evening, in loneliness, circle the lantern."

Furious, I wrote out verses. Despite the fact that I had never in my life written haiku or the like, I churned out poems, dozens of them. At last, exhausted, I laid my head down on Sensei's futon and sprawled out on the tatami. My eyelids closed, and I was powerless to open them. I was barely conscious of my body being dragged (it must have been

Sensei doing the dragging) to lie in the middle of the futon, but when I awoke, I could still hear the sound of the waves, and light shone through the opening in the curtains.

Feeling a bit cramped in, I glanced around and found Sensei sleeping beside me. I had been sleeping against his arm as a pillow. I let out a little cry and sat up. Then, without thinking, I fled back to my room. I dove under the covers of my own futon, then quickly leapt back out, paced circles around the room—opening the curtains, closing the curtains—before diving back under the covers and pulling the quilt up over my head. Then, leaping from the futon once again and with my mind totally blank, I returned to Sensei's room. Sensei was waiting for me there, eyes wide open but still in bed in the dimly lit room with the curtains drawn.

"Tsukiko, there you are," Sensei said softly as he moved to the edge of the futon.

Yes, I said quietly, diving under the covers. The sense of Sensei washed over me. Sensei, I said, burying my face in his chest. Sensei kissed my hair again and again. He touched my breasts over my *yukata*, and then not over my *yukata*.

"Such lovely breasts," Sensei said. His tone was the same as when he had been explaining Basho's poetry. I chuckled, and so did Sensei.

"Such lovely breasts. Such a lovely girl you are, Tsukiko," Sensei said as he caressed my face. He caressed my face, over and over. His caresses made me sleepy. I'm going to fall asleep, Sensei, I said, and he replied, Then go to sleep.

I don't want to sleep, I murmured, but I couldn't keep my eyes open any longer. It was as if his palms had some kind of hypnotic effect. I don't want to sleep. I want to stay here in your arms, I tried to say, but I couldn't get the words out. I don't want to . . . don't want to . . . don't want . . . to . . . , at last my utterances broke apart. At some point, Sensei's hand stopping moving as well. I could hear his light sleeping breath. Sensei, I said, summoning the last of my strength.

Tsukiko, Sensei seemed to rouse himself in reply.

As I drifted off to sleep, I could faintly hear the seagulls' cries above the sea. Sensei, don't go to sleep, I tried to say, but I couldn't. I was being pulled down into a deep sleep, there within Sensei's arms. I gave in to it. I let myself be dragged down into my own slumber, far removed from Sensei's slumber. The seagulls called out their cries in the morning light.

The Tidal Flat—Dream

I THOUGHT I heard a rustling murmur. It was the camphor tree outside the window. Come here, it sounded like, or Who are you? I stuck my head out the open window to look and see. A number of small birds were flitting about among the branches of the camphor tree. They were fast, and I couldn't catch sight of them. I only knew they were there because the leaves moved around them as they fluttered about.

In the cherry trees in Sensei's garden, I'd seen birds before, come to think of it. It was nighttime. The birds would flap their wings a few times and then settle down. These little birds in the camphor tree, they weren't settling down at all. They just kept fluttering about. And the camphor tree kept murmuring, Come here.

I hadn't seen Sensei for some time now. Even when I went to Satoru's place, I still did not come across him sitting there at the counter.

As I listened to the murmur of the branches of the camphor tree, Come here, I decided to go back to Satoru's that night. Broad beans were now out of season, but surely the first edamame would have arrived. The little birds continued their flitting about, rustling the greenery.

"*HIYA-YAKKO*," I ORDERED chilled tofu from my seat at the end of the counter. Sensei wasn't here. He wasn't seated on the tatami or at one of the tables either.

Even after I drank down my beer and switched to saké, Sensei still did not appear. The thought of going to his house occurred to me, but that would be presumptuous. While I sat there, distractedly in my cups, I started to grow tired.

I went into the bathroom, and while I sat there, I looked out the small window. As I did my business, I mused that there must be a poem about how depressing it is to look out the window in a toilet and see blue sky. I would say that a window in a toilet would definitely make you depressed.

Maybe I should go to Sensei's house after all, I was thinking to myself as I came out of the bathroom, and there was Sensei, sitting up straight as usual in the seat two over from mine.

"Here you are, *hiya-yakko*," Satoru said as Sensei took the bowl he passed over the counter. Sensei carefully doused it with soy sauce. Gently, he picked some of the tofu with his chopsticks and brought it to his lips.

"It's tasty," Sensei said straightaway, facing me. Without any greeting or introduction, he spoke as if continuing a conversation we had been having all along.

"I ate some earlier myself," I said, and Sensei nodded lightly.

"Tofu is quite special."

"Yes."

"It's good warm. It's good chilled. It's good boiled. It's good fried. It's versatile," Sensei said readily, taking a sip from the small saké cup.

C'mon, Sensei, let's have a drink, it's been a long time, I said, filling his cup.

All right, Tsukiko, let's have a drink then. Sensei poured for me in return.

We drank quite heavily that night. More heavily than we'd ever drunk before.

ARE THOSE BOATS out at sea, there, what look like needles lined up along the horizon? Sensei and I fixed our gaze on them for a moment. My eyes got dry as I stared out at them. I quickly lost interest, but Sensei's gaze was interminably steady.

"Sensei, aren't you hot?" I asked, but he shook his head.

I wondered where we were. Was this a dream? I had been drinking with Sensei. I had lost count of how many empty saké bottles there had been.

"Must be littleneck clams," Sensei murmured, shifting his gaze from the horizon to the tidal flat. There were lots of people gathering shellfish in the shallows.

"They're out of season, but I wonder if you can still find them around here," Sensei continued.

"Sensei, where are we?" I asked.

"We're back again," was all Sensei said in reply.

Back again? I asked, and Sensei repeated, Yes, back again. I find myself here sometimes.

"I prefer the common clam to littleneck clams," Sensei went on brightly, interrupting me as I was about to ask where this place was that he sometimes went to.

"Oh, I like littlenecks," I replied, caught up in his enthusiasm. Seabirds rustled and flew about. Very carefully, Sensei set down the to-go glass of saké he had been holding atop a rock. There was still about half left.

"Tsukiko, please, have some if you like," Sensei said. I looked down and was surprised to see that I too was holding a to-go glass of saké. Its contents were almost gone, though.

"When you're finished drinking that, do you mind if I use the glass as an ashtray?" Sensei asked, and I hastily finished off the rest.

"Much obliged," Sensei took the glass from me and tapped the ash from his cigarette into it. Thin wisps of cloud hung in the sky. Every so often, children's voices echoed up from the tidal flat. I thought I heard one of them say, Look what a big one I dug up!

"Where are we?"

"I don't really know," Sensei replied, casting his eyes toward the sea.

"Have we left Satoru's place?"

"Probably not."

"Huh?"

I was surprised by how loudly my own voice echoed. Sensei was still looking off at the sea. The wind was damp and smelled like the ocean.

"Sometimes I find myself here, but this is the first time I've ever come here with someone else," Sensei squinted.

"But it's probably just a matter of convincing myself that we came here together."

The sun was strong. The seabirds rustled as they flew about. I could probably imagine that it sounded like Come here. At some point, my hand was clasped around a to-go glass of saké. It was filled to the brim. I quaffed it in one swig, but I didn't feel the least bit drunk. It's that kind of place, Sensei said as if to himself.

"Hey . . . ," Sensei said. As he spoke, his profile seemed to blur.

"What's the matter?" I asked, and Sensei looked sad.

"I'll be sure to come back again," he said, and then simply disappeared. The cigarette he had been smoking had vanished. I wandered a few meters around in each direction, but he was gone. I even looked behind the rocks, but he wasn't there either. I gave up and sat down on a rock, gulping down the saké. If you set down an empty bottle on the rocks, it would disappear in the blink of an eye. The same way that Sensei had disappeared. It must be that kind of place. I kept drinking as many glasses of saké as sprang up in my hand, while I looked off toward the sea.

JUST AS HE'D promised, Sensei reappeared momentarily later.

"How many have you had?" he said as he came up from behind me.

"Hmm . . . ," I *was* a little drunk. Even in "that kind" of place, when you drank that much, I guess you could still feel the effects.

"Well, I'm back," Sensei said curtly.

"Did you go back to Satoru's place?" I asked, and Sensei shook his head.

"I went home."

"Really? Huh, I wouldn't have thought."

"Drunkenness brings out the homing instinct," Sensei said solemnly. I laughed, and at that moment the contents of my saké glass spilled out onto the rocks.

"The empty glass, if you will." Just as he had before, Sensei held a cigarette. At the bar, he rarely if ever smoked, but I suppose when he came here, he always smoked. He tapped the ash into the glass just as it was about to fall off.

Most of the people on the tidal flat were wearing hats. Their heads covered, they squatted as they dug for shellfish. Short shadows sprouted from each of their haunches. They were all facing the same direction as they dug.

"I wonder why they enjoy doing that," Sensei said while he carefully stubbed out his cigarette on the edge of the glass.

"What do you mean?"

"Digging for shellfish."

All of a sudden, right there on the rocks, Sensei started doing a headstand. The rocks were at an angle, so that Sensei's headstand was aslant. He wobbled a little, but he soon steadied.

"Maybe they plan to have them for dinner," I replied.

"You mean, eat them?" Sensei's voice drifted up from my feet.

"Or maybe they'll keep them."

"Keep the littleneck clams?"

"When I was little, I had a pet snail."

"A pet snail is not particularly unusual."

"Isn't it the same? They're shellfish."

"Now, Tsukiko, are snails shellfish?"

"No, I guess not."

He was still standing on his head. But I didn't think it was strange at all. It must be this place. Then I remembered something. It was about Sensei's wife. I had never met her, however, I must have been remembering on behalf of Sensei.

His wife was very good at magic. She started with basic sleight of hand like manipulating a red ball between her fingertips, then moved on to large-scale tricks that involved animals, until her skills were really like that of a professional. But she did not perform her tricks for anyone. She would only practice them alone at home. Every so often, she might demonstrate a newly learned trick to Sensei, but that was rare. He was vaguely aware that she practiced diligently during the day, but he wondered just how much. He knew that she raised rabbits and pigeons in cages, but these animals for magic tricks were smaller and more passive than usual. Even though she kept them inside the house, you could easily forget they were there.

Once, Sensei had an errand that took him to the busy shopping district, far from school, and as he was walking along, a woman who, from straight on, looked just like his wife was headed toward him. However, her carriage and attire differed from his wife's usual appearance. This woman was wearing a gaudy dress that bared her shoulders. She was arm in arm with a bearded man in a flashy suit who did not seem like the type who made an honest living. Sensei's wife may have been willful at times, but she did not care to be the center of attention. That being the case, he figured it couldn't be his wife, it must just be someone who looks like her, and he looked away.

His wife's doppelgänger and the bearded man were quickly approaching. Sensei had already looked away, yet he found his gaze drawn to the couple once again. The woman was smiling. Her smile was exactly like his wife's smile. And as she grinned, she pulled a pigeon from her pocket, which she then perched on Sensei's shoulder. Then she took a small rabbit from her bodice, and placed it on his other shoulder. The rabbit was as still as if it were a figurine. Sensei too stood still, transfixed. Lastly the woman drew a monkey out from beneath her skirt and saddled it on Sensei's back.

"How ya doing, dear?" the woman said sunnily.

"Is that you, Sumiyo?"

"Shush!" Instead of replying to Sensei's question, the woman scolded the thrashing pigeon. The pigeon soon settled down. The bearded man and the woman were holding each other's hand tightly. Sensei gently set the rabbit and the pigeon down on the ground, but he struggled with how to handle the monkey clinging to his back. The man drew the woman closer to him, and then, putting his arm around her shoulder, he whisked her away. They just rushed off, while Sensei was stuck dealing with the monkey.

"Your wife's name was Sumiyo, wasn't it?" I asked.

Sensei nodded. "Sumiyo was a peculiar woman, indeed."

"I see."

"After she left home, more than fifteen years ago, she moved around from one place to another. Even still, she would regularly send me postcards. Dutifully."

Sensei was no longer standing on his head; now he was sitting on his heels with his legs folded under him on the rocks. He had called his own wife a strange woman. However, here on the tidal flat, Sensei was the one behaving quite strangely.

"The last postcard, which arrived five years ago, had a postmark from the island you and I went to recently."

There were more people on the tidal flat. With their backsides facing us, they were digging for shellfish intently. I heard children's voices. They sounded long and drawn-out, like a tape that was being played back too slowly.

Sensei closed his eyes as he blew cigarette smoke into the empty saké glass. I was able to recall with such detail things about Sensei's wife—whom I had never met—but when I thought about myself, I could remember nothing. There were only the glimmering boats heading out to sea.

"What kind of place is this?"

"It seems like some sort of middle place."

"Middle place?"

"Perhaps like a borderline."

A borderline between what? Did Sensei really come to a place like this all the time? I gulped down another glassful of saké, with no idea how many I'd had, and looked out at the tidal flat. The figures there were hazy and blurred.

"Our dog," Sensei began, setting down his empty glass on the rocks. The glass suddenly disappeared before my eyes.

We had a dog. It must have been when my son was still small. A Shiba Inu. I love Shibas. My wife liked mutts. She once brought home a bizarre-looking dog from somewhere—it looked like a cross between a dachshund and a bulldog—and that dog lived a very long time. My wife loved that dog. But we had the Shiba before that one. The Shiba ate something he shouldn't have, then he was ill for a short time, and in the end he died. My son was devastated. I was sad too. But my wife didn't shed a single tear. Rather, she seemed almost resentful. Resentful at our weepy son and at me.

After we buried the Shiba in our garden, suddenly my wife said to our son, "It's all right, he'll be reincarnated."

She went on, "Chiro will soon be reincarnated."

"But what will he be reincarnated as?" our son must have asked, his eyes swollen from crying.

"He'll be reincarnated as me."

"Huh?!?" our son said, eyes agog. I too was stunned. What could this woman possibly mean? There was no rhyme or reason to it, nor was it any consolation.

"Mom, don't say such weird things," our son said, a note of anger in his voice.

"It's not weird," Sumiyo sniffed, and hurried inside the house. A few days passed without any incident but, I think it was less than a week later, we were at the dinner table when suddenly Sumiyo started barking.

"*Arf*" was the sound she made. Chiro had a high-pitched bark. She sounded exactly like him. Perhaps because she had studied magic tricks, she may have been cleverer than most people at mimicry, but nevertheless, she sounded exactly like him.

"Quit your stupid joke," I said, but Sumiyo paid no attention. For the rest of the meal, she continued to bark. *Arf, arf, arf.* Both our son and I lost our appetites and quickly got up from the table.

The next day Sumiyo was back to her usual self, but our son was infuriated. Mom, say you're sorry, he demanded persistently. Sumiyo was completely indifferent.

But he's been reincarnated. Chiro's inside me now. The casual way in which she said it only intensified his pique. Ultimately, neither one of them would concede to the other. This was the source of the strained relationship between them, and after our son graduated from high school, he decided to go off to a faraway university, and he stayed there and found a job. He rarely visited, even after his own child was born.

I would ask Sumiyo, Don't you love your grandchild? Don't you have any desire to see him?

"Not particularly," she would say.

Then, Sumiyo disappeared.

· · ·

"So, THEN, WHERE are we?" I asked, for the umpteenth time. And still, Sensei did not reply.

Perhaps Sumiyo couldn't bear misfortune. Perhaps she couldn't stand feeling unhappy.

"Sensei," I called out. "You cared deeply for Sumiyo, didn't you?"

Sensei made a harrumphing sound and glared at me. "Whether I cared for her or not, she was a selfish woman."

"Was she?"

"Selfish, headstrong, and temperamental."

"They all mean the same thing."

"Yes, they do."

The tidal flat was now completely obscured by haze. Where we were, the place where Sensei and I stood, to-go glasses of saké in hand, appeared to be nothing but air, all around us.

"Where are we?"

"This place is, well, here."

Once in a while, children's voices would rise up from below. The voices were sluggish and distant.

"We were young, Sumiyo and I."

"You're still young."

"That's not what I meant."

"Sensei, I've had enough of these glasses of saké."

"Shall we go down there and dig for littleneck clams?"

"We can't eat them raw."

"We could build a fire and roast them."

"Roast them?"

"You're right, it's too much trouble."

Something made a rustling sound. It was the camphor tree murmuring outside my window. This was a pleasant time of year. It rained often, but the rain-slicked leaves on the camphor tree gleamed lustrously. Sensei smoked his cigarette somewhat distractedly.

This place is a borderline. Sensei seemed to have moved his lips, but in fact, I couldn't tell if he had spoken or not.

"How long have you been coming here?" I asked, and Sensei smiled.

"Perhaps since around when I was your age. Somehow I just had to urge to come here."

Sensei, let's go back to Satoru's place. I don't want to stay in this strange place anymore. Let's hurry back, I called out to Sensei. Let's go back.

But how do we get out of this place? Sensei replied.

A flurry of voices rose up from the tidal flat. The camphor tree outside the window made a rustling murmur. Sensei and I stood there in a daze, to-go glasses of saké in our hands. The leaves of the camphor tree outside my window murmured, Come here.

The Cricket

LATELY, FOR A while now, I haven't seen Sensei.

And it's not because we ended up in that strange place together—it's because I'm avoiding him.

I don't go anywhere near Satoru's place. I don't take evening walks on my days off either. Instead of wandering around the old market in the shopping district, I hurriedly do my shopping at the big supermarket by the station. I don't go to the used bookstore or the two bookshops in the neighborhood. I figure if I can manage not to do these things, than maybe I won't run into Sensei. Should be easy.

Easy enough that I could probably manage not to see Sensei for the rest of my life. And if I never saw him again, then maybe I could move on.

"It grows because you plant it." This was a phrase often repeated by my great-aunt when she was alive. As old as she was, my great-aunt was still more enlightened than my own mother. After her husband, my great-uncle, passed away, she had numerous "boyfriends" who doted on her as she dashed around to dinners and card games and croquet.

"That's how love is," she used to say. "If the love is true, then treat it the same way you would a plant—fertilize it, protect it from the

elements—you must do absolutely everything you can. But if it isn't
true, then it's best to just let it wither on the vine."

My great-aunt was fond of wordplay and puns.

If I followed her theory, and didn't see Sensei for a long time, then
maybe my feelings for him would just wither away.

Which was why I've been avoiding him lately.

IF I LEFT my apartment and walked for a while alongside the big main
road, then followed a street that led into a residential area before reaching the riverside, if I walked about one hundred meters further, there on
the corner was Sensei's house.

Sensei's house was not on the riverfront; it was set back about
three houses from the water. Up until about thirty years ago, whenever a big typhoon came through, the easily overflowing river would
flood the neighborhood up to the houses' floorboards. During the era of
rapid economic growth, there were large-scale river improvements that
enclosed the riverbank in concrete. The wall was dug quite deep, which
also widened the river.

It used to be a swiftly flowing river. The water moved so fast you
could barely tell if it was transparent or muddy. There must have been
something inviting about the current, because occasionally people would
throw themselves into it. Most of the time, though, instead of drowning
they would be carried downstream and then rescued, to their dismay, or
so I heard.

On my days off it had been my habit—not necessarily with the
intention of running into Sensei—to stroll along the river on my way to
the market by the station. However, if I was trying not to see him, then
I ought not to stroll at all. This put me at a loss as to how to spend my
leisure time.

For a while, I tried taking the train to go see a movie or going
downtown to shop for clothes or shoes.

But I simply felt out of sorts. The weekend cinema that smelled like popcorn, the stale air of a brightly lit department store on a summer evening, the chilly bustle at the register of a big bookstore—it was all too much for me. I felt as if I couldn't breathe.

I even tried taking weekend trips on my own. I bought a book, *Suburban Hot Spring Hotels: Travel Without an Itinerary*, and proceeded to visit several of these places "itinerantly."

Times had changed—nowadays, hotels didn't seem to consider a woman traveling alone unusual. They briskly escorted me to my room, briskly instructed me where the dining room and the bath were located, and briskly indicated when checkout time was.

I had no other choice, and once I had briskly used the bath, briskly finished my dinner, and briskly taken another bath, there was nothing else to do. I briskly went to bed, briskly left the next morning, and that was all there was to it.

Up until now, I thought I had enjoyed my life alone, somehow.

I quickly lost interest in the "itinerant" travel, and seeing as how I couldn't take evening walks by the river, I sprawled around my apartment, thinking to myself.

But had I really enjoyed living life on my own until now?

Joyful. Painful. Pleasant. Sweet. Bitter. Sour. Ticklish. Itchy. Cold. Hot. Lukewarm.

Just what kind of life had I lived? I wondered.

While I contemplated these things, I became sleepy. Since I was already sprawled on the floor, my eyes soon grew heavy.

Resting on a cushion I had folded in half, I slipped off into sleep. A gentle breeze drifted in through the screen door and washed over me. Off in the distance, I could hear the hum of cicadas.

But why was I avoiding Sensei? I wondered, on the verge of sleep, the stray thought arriving drowsily, like in a dream. In my dream, I was walking on a dusty white road. Where was Sensei? I looked for him, the cicadas' call raining down on me from above as I kept walking along the white road.

I couldn't seem to find Sensei.

That's right, I had put him away in a box. Now I remembered.

I had wrapped Sensei neatly in a piece of silk cloth with French seams and put him into a big paulownia wood box, which I then tucked away in the closet.

I couldn't take Sensei back out now. The closet was too deep. And the silk cloth was so nice and cool, Sensei would want to stay wrapped up in it. He would just keep dozing in the dusk inside the box.

I kept stride along the white road while I thought about Sensei, lying in the box with his eyes open. The cicadas bombarded me from above with their maddening drone.

I saw Takashi Kojima for the first time in a while. He told me that he had been away on a month-long business trip. He had brought me back a heavy metal nutcracker "as a souvenir," he said.

"Where did you go?" I asked, opening and closing the nutcracker.

"Here and there around the western part of the States," Kojima replied.

"Here and there?" I smiled as I repeated his words, and Kojima smiled too.

"Towns whose name I'm sure you've never heard of, sweetheart."

I pretended not to notice that he had called me sweetheart.

"What kind of work were you doing in these towns that I haven't heard of?"

"Oh, well, this and that."

Kojima's arms were tanned.

"Looks like you got some American sun," I said, and Kojima nodded.

"But if you think about it, there is no such thing as American sun or Japanese sun. There's only one sun, of course."

I stared distractedly at Kojima's arms while snapping the

nutcracker open and shut. There's only one sun, of course. I could imagine my mind spinning off from his words and getting all sentimental, but I stopped myself.

"Lately, you know . . ."

"Yeah?"

"I've been itinerant, this summer."

"Itinerant?"

"Yes, itinerant, going here and there."

How genteel, I envy you, Kojima said without hesitation.

Oh, yes, quite genteel, I replied, just as readily.

In the ambient lighting of Bar Maeda, the nutcracker shone dully. Kojima and I each drank two bourbon and sodas. We paid our bill and climbed the stairs. Standing on the top step, lightly but formally, we shook hands. Then, lightly but formally, we kissed.

"You seem like you're somewhere else," Kojima said.

"Like I said, I've been itinerant lately," I replied, and Kojima tilted his head.

"What does that mean, sweetheart?"

"The 'sweetheart' bit sounds quite odd to me."

"I don't think so," Kojima said.

"I do," I retorted, and Kojima laughed.

"Summer will be over soon."

"Yes, soon it will be."

We shook hands again, formally, and then went our separate ways.

"Tsukiko, it's been a while," Satoru said.

It was already past ten o'clock. This was about the time for last call at Satoru's place. I hadn't been there in two months.

I was on my way home from a farewell party for my boss, who was retiring. Even drunker than usual, I was feeling uninhibited. *It's been two months, everything should be all right*, my inebriated mind told me.

"It's been a long time." My voice sounded more high-pitched than usual.

"What can I get you?" Satoru asked, looking up from his chopping block.

"Chilled saké. And edamame."

"All right, then," Satoru replied, looking down again at the chopping block.

There were no other customers at the counter. The only other people were two couples sitting quietly across from each other at the tables.

I sipped the chilled saké. Satoru was silent. The baseball scores were on the radio broadcast.

"The Giants came from behind, huh," Satoru muttered, as if to himself. I scanned around the bar. There were a few forgotten umbrellas in the umbrella stand. It hadn't rained at all for the past several days.

A chirping rose up from the area around my feet. I had thought the noise was part of the sports broadcast, but now it seemed like the sound of an insect. *Chirp, chirp,* it called. Then it would stop. Just when you thought it was done, the chirping would start up again.

"There's an insect . . . ," I said when Satoru handed me a steaming plate of edamame.

"Must be a cricket. It's been there since this morning," Satoru replied.

"You mean here inside the bar?"

"Yeah, it seems like one got in somewhere around the concrete drain."

The cricket's chirping was almost keeping time with Satoru's voice.

"Sensei said he had a cold. I wonder if he's all right."

"What?"

"He came in last week, in the early evening, with a hell of a cough. And I haven't seen him since," Satoru said, chopping on his block.

"He hasn't been in at all?" I asked. My voice was unpleasantly shrill. It sounded to me like someone else talking.

"Nope."

The cricket was chirping. I could hear the thumping of my own heartbeat. I sat and listened to the sound of blood coursing through my body. The palpitations gradually quickened.

"I wonder if he's all right." Satoru glanced at me. I remained silent, not answering him.

The cricket kept chirping, then it stopped. My racing heartbeat, however, did not subside. It echoed loudly inside my head.

Satoru kept chopping away with his knife on his block, interminably. The cricket started up its chirping again.

I KNOCKED ON the door.

This was after I had paced around in front of Sensei's gate for more than ten minutes.

When I went to ring the bell, my fingers froze like ice. So I went around the garden and tried to look in from the veranda, but the rain shutters were closed up tight.

I listened through the shutters for a sign of life, but there was no sound whatsoever. I went around to the back where a light was on low in the kitchen, and I felt somewhat relieved.

"Sensei," I called out through the front door, but of course there was no reply. How could he reply if he had no voice left to call out with?

"Sensei," I said several more times, but my voice was swallowed up by the night's darkness. That's why I was knocking on the door.

I heard footsteps in the hall.

"Who is it?" a voice asked, hoarsely.

"It's me."

"'It's me' is not an appropriate response, Tsukiko."

"But you know who it is, don't you?"

During this exchange, the door screeched open. Sensei stood there, wearing striped pajama pants and a T-shirt that said I □ NY.

"What's the matter?" Sensei asked with perfect composure.

"Um."

"A lady doesn't go visit a man in the middle of the night."

He was the same old Sensei. The moment I looked him in the eye, my knees went weak.

"What do you mean? You're the one who invites me over here whenever you're drunk."

"I'm not the least bit drunk tonight."

He spoke as if we'd been together all evening. Suddenly I felt as if the two months I had been distancing myself from Sensei never happened.

"Satoru said you were sick."

"I had a cold but I'm quite well now."

"Why are you wearing that strange T-shirt?"

"It's a hand-me-up from my grandson."

Sensei and I held each other's gaze. Sensei's beard was unshaven. His whiskers were white.

"By the way, Tsukiko, long time no see."

Sensei narrowed his eyes. But he didn't look away, so neither could I. Sensei smiled. Awkwardly, I smiled back.

"Sensei."

"What is it, Tsukiko?"

"You're just fine, aren't you?"

"Did you think I was dead?"

"The thought might have crossed my mind."

Sensei laughed out loud. I laughed too. But our laughter fell silent as soon as it converged. *Please don't say the word "dead," Sensei,* I wanted to plead. *But Tsukiko, everyone dies. And what's more, at my age I'm much more likely to die that you are. It stands to reason.* I had no trouble imagining his response.

The specter of death always loomed over us.

Come in for a while, Sensei said. Have some tea, he said as he led the way inside. The small I □ NY logo was also printed on the back of Sensei's T-shirt. I read it aloud while I took off my shoes.

So, you wear pajamas, Sensei? I would have thought you wore *nemaki*, I muttered as I trailed after him, referring to Japanese-style sleepwear.

Sensei turned to face me. Tsukiko, please refrain from commenting about my clothing choices.

Yes, I answered quietly.

Very well, then, Sensei replied.

The interior of the house was damp and quiet. A futon was laid out in the tatami room. Sensei took his time making the tea and he took his time serving it to me. For my part, I lingered over my cup, drawing out the minutes.

Several times, I called out, "Sensei," and each time, Sensei would reply, "What is it?" I wouldn't say anything in response, until the next time I called out, "Sensei." It was all I could manage.

Once I had finished drinking my tea, I took my leave.

"Please take good care of yourself." I bowed politely at the front door.

"Tsukiko." This time Sensei was the one to call my name.

"Yes?" I raised my head, looking Sensei in the eye. His cheeks were sunken and his hair was tousled.

"Get home safely," Sensei said after a moment's pause.

"I'll be fine," I replied, rapping on my chest.

I CLOSED THE front door to prevent Sensei from walking me to the gate. A half-moon hung in the sky. Dozens of insects were chirping and buzzing in the garden.

I'm so confused, I muttered, leaving Sensei's house.

I don't care anymore. About love or anything. It doesn't matter what happens.

In truth, it really didn't matter. As long as Sensei was fine and well, that's what was important.

This was enough. I would stop hoping for anything from Sensei, I thought to myself as I walked along the road by the river.

The river flowed along, silently, to the sea. I wondered if right now Sensei was nestled in bed, in his T-shirt and his pajama pants. Was his house locked up properly? Had he turned out the light in the kitchen? And checked the gas?

"Sensei," I breathed his name softly, in lieu of a sigh.

"Sensei."

The air rising off the river carried a crisp hint of autumn. Goodnight, Sensei. You looked quite nice in your I □ NY T-shirt. Once you're all better, let's go for drink. Fall is here, so at Satoru's place there will be warm things to eat while we drink.

Turning to face toward Sensei, who was now several hundred meters away, I kept on speaking to him. I walked along the length of the river, as if I were having a conversation with the moon. I kept talking, as if forever.

In the Park

....

I WAS ASKED out on a date. By Sensei.

I find it awkward to use the word "date," despite the fact that the two of us had gone on that trip together (though, of course, we hadn't actually been "together"), but we had plans to go to an art museum to see an exhibit of ancient calligraphy, which may sound like the kind of thing students would do on a school trip, yet nevertheless, it was a date. Sensei himself had been the one to say, "Tsukiko, let's go on a date."

It had not been in the drunken fervor at Satoru's place. It had not been a coincidental meeting on the street. Nor did it seem to be because he happened to have two tickets. Sensei had called me up (however it was that he got my phone number) and, straightforward and to the point, he had said, "Let's go on a date." Sensei's voice had a more mellow resonance over the phone. Perhaps it was because the sound was slightly muted.

We arranged to meet on Saturday in the early afternoon. Not at the station near here but rather in front of the station where the art museum was, two train lines away. Apparently, Sensei would be busy with something all morning but would then head toward the station by the art museum.

"It's such a big station that I'm a bit worried about you getting lost, Tsukiko," Sensei laughed on the other end of the line.

"I won't get lost. I'm not a little girl anymore," I said, and then, not knowing what else to say, I fell silent. On the phone with Kojima (we had spoken on the phone more often than we had seen each other), I had always been so relaxed, yet talking to Sensei now, I felt terribly ill at ease. When we were sitting next to each other in the bar, watching Satoru as he moved about, if the conversation lulled, it didn't matter how long the silence lasted. But on the phone, silence yawned like a void.

Um. Yes. Well. These were the catalog of sounds I uttered while on the phone with Sensei. My voice got smaller and smaller and, although I was happy to hear from Sensei, all I could think about was how soon could I get off the phone.

"Well, then, I'm looking forward to our date, Tsukiko," Sensei said in closing.

Yes, I replied in a faint voice. Saturday afternoon, at the ticket gate. One thirty, sharp. Rain or shine. So, I'll see you then. Good day.

After the call ended, I sat sprawled on the floor. Soon there was a soft blare from the receiver I still held in my hand. But I just sat there, not moving.

ON SATURDAY, THE weather was clear. The day was warm for fall, so warm that even my not-so-thick long-sleeved shirt felt too heavy. I had learned my lesson on our recent trip, and decided against wearing anything that I wasn't comfortable in, like a dress or high heels. I wore a long-sleeved shirt over cotton pants, with loafers. I knew Sensei would probably say I was dressed like a boy, but so what.

I had given up worrying about Sensei's intentions. I wouldn't get attached. I wouldn't distance us. He would be gentlemanly. I would be ladylike. A mild acquaintance. That's what I had decided. Slightly, for the long term, and without expectations. No matter how I tried to get closer to him, Sensei would not let me near. As if there were an invisible wall between us. It might have seemed pliant and obscure, but when compressed it could withstand anything, nothing could get through. A wall made of air.

The day was quite sunny. Starlings were huddled close together on the electrical wires. I had thought they only gathered like that at dusk, but there were flocks of them lined up on the electrical wires all around, and it was still early in the day. I wondered what they were saying to each other in bird language.

"They do make a ruckus, don't they?" Suddenly a voice seemed to come down from above—it was Sensei. He was wearing a dark brown jacket, with a plain beige cotton shirt over light brown trousers. Sensei was always rather smartly dressed. He would never wear anything trendy like a bolo tie.

"Looks like fun," I said. Sensei gazed up at the flock of starlings for a moment. Then he looked at me and smiled.

"Shall we go?" he said.

Yes, I replied, my gaze downward. All he had said was "Shall we go?" in the same voice as always, but I felt strangely emotional.

Sensei paid for our admission. When I tried to hand him money, he shook his head. No, please, I invited you, he said, refusing to take it.

We entered the art museum together. It was surprisingly crowded inside. I was amazed that so many people could be interested in completely indecipherable calligraphy from the Heian and Kamakura eras. Sensei stared through the glass at the rolled letter papers and hanging scrolls. I watched Sensei's back.

"Tsukiko, isn't this simply lovely?" Sensei was pointing at what appeared to be a letter with fluttery script written in pale ink. I couldn't make out a word.

"Sensei, can you read this?"

"Ah, actually, I can't really," Sensei said with a laugh. "But still, it really is a nice hand."

Do you think so?

"Tsukiko, when you see a handsome man, even if you cannot understand what he says, you still think, 'Oh, that guy's good-looking,' don't you? Handwriting is the same."

I see, I nodded. Did that mean when Sensei saw an attractive woman, he thought, "Oh, what a pretty girl"?

After looking at the special exhibition on the second floor, we went back downstairs to view the permanent collection, and by then two hours had passed.

The calligraphy was utter gibberish to me, but I found myself enjoying the time as I listened to Sensei's murmured bursts of "Such a nice hand" or "A bit prosaic" or "Now that's what's called a vigorous style." The same way as when you're sitting at a sidewalk café, furtively passing judgment on people as you watch them go by, it was amusing to attach my own impressions to these calligraphed works from the Heian or Kamakura eras: "That's nice" or "This one's not bad" or "It reminds me of a guy I used to go out with."

Sensei and I sat down on a sofa on the staircase's landing. Numerous people passed before us. Tsukiko, was that boring for you? Sensei asked.

No, it was rather interesting, I replied, staring at the backsides of the people passing by. I could feel the warmth radiating from Sensei's body. The stirring of emotion returned. The hard sofa with bad springs felt like the most comfortable thing in the world. I was happy to be here like this with Sensei. I was simply happy.

"Tsukiko, is something wrong?" Sensei asked, peering at my face.

Walking alongside Sensei, I had been muttering to myself, "Hopes strictly forbidden, hopes strictly forbidden." I was mimicking the main character in the book *The Flying Classroom*, which I read when I was little, who says, "Crying strictly forbidden, crying strictly forbidden."

This may have been the closest I had ever walked beside Sensei. Usually Sensei stood in front of me, or I darted out quickly—one or the other.

If someone were walking toward us, we would each break off to the left or to the right to make room for the person to pass. Once they had gone by, we would resume walking closely side by side.

"Don't go to the other side, Tsukiko, come my way," Sensei said after the umpteenth person headed toward us. But I still broke off from Sensei and went "to the other side." For some reason, I just wouldn't huddle over with Sensei.

"Stop swinging around like a pendulum." Sensei suddenly grabbed my arm as I started for "the other side." He tugged firmly. It wasn't that he used that much force, but since I had been moving away from him, it felt like I was being tugged.

"Let's walk alongside each other," Sensei said, still holding my arm.

Yes, I replied, looking downward. I was about a thousand times more nervous than the first time I had gone on a date with a boy. We kept walking along, Sensei still holding my arm. The trees lining the street were just barely starting to show their autumn colors. *It looks like he's bringing me in for questioning*, I thought as I walked beside Sensei.

The art museum was located within a big park. To the left, there was another museum and to the right was a zoo. The late afternoon sunlight shone on Sensei's torso. A child was scattering popcorn on the path. The moment he dropped the pieces, dozens of pigeons would flock over. The child let out cries of wonder. The pigeons flew around him, even trying to peck at the popcorn that was still in his palm. The boy stood motionless, half crying.

"They're rather aggressive pigeons, aren't they?" Sensei said serenely. Shall we have a seat here? he asked as he sat on a bench. I sat down a moment after Sensei did. Now the afternoon sun's rays fell across my torso as well.

"I bet that boy is about to start wailing," Sensei said, leaning forward with great interest.

"I don't think so."

"No, lots of little boys are crybabies."

"It's not the other way around?"

"No, little boys are much wimpier than little girls."

"Sensei, were you a wimp when you were little?"

"I'm still very much a wimp, even now."

Sure enough, the little boy burst into tears. One of the pigeons had gone so far as to rest on top of his head. A woman who must have been his mother laughed as she came to pick him up.

"Tsukiko," Sensei said, turning toward me. Now that he was facing me, however, I became incapable of facing him.

"Tsukiko, thank you for coming with me to the island that time."

I muttered in reply. I hadn't really wanted to think about what happened on the island. Ever since then the phrase "Hopes strictly forbidden, hopes strictly forbidden," had been echoing in my mind.

"I've always been, well, a shilly-shallier."

"A shilly-shallier?"

"Isn't that what they used to call a kid who's slow to respond or do something?"

But Sensei didn't seem like the kind of person who shilly-shallied. I always thought of him as briskly decisive, standing up straight.

"No, in this way I am really something of a shilly-shallier."

The boy who had been swarmed by the pigeons, now that he was in his mother's arms, started scattering popcorn again.

"The child didn't learn his lesson, did he?"

"Children never do."

"That's right, and I guess I'm no different."

He shilly-shallies and he never learns. Just what was Sensei trying to say? I stole a glance at him—he was sitting up perfectly straight, as always, watching the little boy.

"When we were on the island, I was still shilly-shallying."

The pigeons were swarming the boy again. His mother scolded him. The pigeons were trying to alight on her too. Still holding the boy, she tried to extricate herself from the flock of birds. But since the boy wouldn't stop strewing the popcorn, the pigeons just kept following the mother and child. It looked as though they were trailing a huge moving carpet made of pigeons.

"Tsukiko, how much longer do you think I'll live?" Sensei asked abruptly.

I met Sensei's gaze. His eyes were placid.

"A very, very long time," I cried out reflexively. The young couple sitting on the next bench turned around in surprise. Several pigeons took flight.

"You know that's not the case."

"But, still, a long time."

Sensei took my left hand in his right hand, his dry palm enveloping mine.

"And would you not be satisfied, if it weren't a long time?"

What? My mouth was half-open. Sensei had called himself a shilly-shallier, but I was the one who hesitated now. Even in the midst of this conversation, I sat there pathetic and slack-jawed.

The mother and child had disappeared without my noticing. The sun was starting to set, and the first signs of dusk were creeping up around us.

"Tsukiko!" Sensei said, sticking the tip of his left index finger into my open mouth. Astonished, my automatic reaction was to close my mouth. Sensei nimbly pulled his finger back out before it was caught by my teeth.

"What are you doing?!" I cried out. Sensei chuckled.

"You were in a bit of a daze, Tsukiko."

"I was just thinking about what you said."

"I'm sorry." As he apologized, Sensei drew me into his arms.

As he held me close, it seemed like time stopped.

Sensei, I whispered.

Tsukiko, Sensei whispered back.

"Sensei, even if you were to die very soon, it would be all right for me. I could handle it," I said, pressing my face against his chest.

"I'm not going to die very soon," Sensei replied, still holding me in his arms. His voice was hushed. He sounded just like he had over the telephone: muted, with a mellow timbre.

"It was a rhetorical statement."

"Well, then, rhetorically, it was an apt expression."

"Thank you."

Even as we embraced each other, we continued to speak formally.

One after another, the pigeons were flying up into the cluster of trees. Up above, crows were circling. They cawed loudly to each other. The darkness was gradually deepening. I could only make out the dim outlines of the young couple on the next bench.

"Tsukiko," Sensei said, adjusting himself so that he was sitting upright again.

"Yes?" I too sat up straight.

"So, then, well."

"Yes?"

Sensei fell silent for a moment. I could barely see his face in the twilight. Our bench was the farthest one from the lamppost. Sensei cleared his throat a few times.

"So, then, well."

"Yes?"

"Would you consider a relationship with me, based on a premise of love?"

Excuse me? I stammered in response. What do you mean by that, Sensei? I'm already in love with you, for a while now, I blurted out, forgetting any and all restraint. I've loved you all along, I told you. Sensei, you already know that very well. So what, then, do you mean by this "premise"? I don't get it.

A crow on a nearby branch cawed loudly. Surprised, I flew up off the bench. The crow gave another caw. Sensei smiled. He wrapped his palm around mine again, still smiling.

I clung to him. Wrapping my free arm around Sensei's back, I pressed myself against his body and inhaled the scent of his jacket. It smelled faintly of mothballs.

"Tsukiko, with you so close, I'm embarrassed."

"Even though you were the one holding me just before."

"That was the decision of a lifetime."

"Yes, but you seemed pretty natural about it."

"Well, I was married before."

"And you must not have felt embarrassed to be like this."

"We're in public."

"It's dark now, no one can see."

"They can see."

"They can't."

With my face in Sensei's chest, I had been crying just a little bit. So that he wouldn't notice my tears or hear them in my voice, I kept my face pressed firmly against his jacket and muffled my words. Sensei calmly patted my hair.

A premise of love, yes, certainly. I was still muffling my voice. Let's have a relationship with that premise, I said, muffled.

That's very fortunate, Tsukiko. You're such a lovely girl, dear. Sensei's words were also muffled. How did you like our first date?

I thought it went pretty well, I replied.

Then let's do it again, Sensei said. Darkness fell quietly over us.

Certainly, it's good to have a premise of love.

So, where should we go next?

Maybe Disneyland would be nice.

Desney, you say?

It's Disney, Sensei.

I see, Disney, right. But I'm not so good with crowds.

But I want to go to Disneyland.

Then let's go to Desneyland.

Didn't I tell you it's not Desneyland?

Tsukiko, dear, you are a real stickler.

Darkness surrounded us as we went on talking to each other in our muffled voices. The pigeons and the crows must have returned to their nests. Enveloped in Sensei's warm and dry embrace, I wanted to laugh and I wanted to cry. But I didn't laugh and I didn't cry anymore either. All I did was be still there in Sensei's arms.

I could feel Sensei's heartbeat faintly through his jacket. We remained there, sitting quietly in the darkness.

The Briefcase

UNUSUALLY, I FOUND myself at Satoru's place while it was still daylight.

It was early winter, so for it to still be bright out, it must have been before five o'clock. I had been out on a call and decided to come straight home, without going back to the office. I had finished what I needed to do more quickly than expected and whereas, once, I would have had a look around a department store or somewhere, I decided to head to Satoru's place and see if Sensei would meet me there. That's how it was now that Sensei and I were in an "official relationship" (Sensei's words). Had it been before our "relationship" started, I never would have called Sensei—though I probably still would have come to Satoru's and whiled away the rest of the daylight by myself, enjoying my saké as I wondered, with heart racing, whether Sensei would show up or not.

It wasn't a huge change. The only real difference was whether to sit and wait or not.

"When you put it that way, it makes waiting sound pretty tough, don't you think?" Satoru said, looking up from his chopping on the other side of the counter. When I arrived he had been out in front of the bar watering. He told me that he was still getting ready to open—the curtain outside wasn't even up yet—but he invited me in anyway.

Have a seat over there. We'll open in about half an hour, Satoru said, placing a beer and glass in front of me along with a bottle opener and a little dish of miso paste. You can open it yourself, right? Satoru said as he diligently maneuvered his knife on the chopping block.

"Sometimes waiting is a good thing."

"You think so?"

The beer entered my system. After a little while, I could feel a warmth along the path it coursed through. I took a lick of the miso paste. It was barley miso.

I excused myself in advance, and took my mobile phone out of my bag and dialed Sensei's number. I debated whether to call his home number or his mobile phone number, but decided on his mobile.

Sensei picked up after six rings. He picked up, but there was only silence. Sensei didn't say anything for the first ten seconds or more. Sensei hated mobile phones, citing the subtle lag after your voice went through as his reason.

"I don't have any particular complaints about mobile phones, per se. I find it intriguing to see people who appear to be having a loud conversation with themselves."

"I see."

"But so then, if we're talking about me agreeing to use a mobile phone, that's a difficult one."

This was the conversation we had when I suggested that Sensei get a mobile phone.

Whereas once, he would have flatly refused to carry a mobile phone, because I had insisted on the idea, he couldn't reject it out of hand. I remember a boy I dated a long time ago who, when we would disagree, would go straight to outright denial, but Sensei wasn't like that. Is that what you called benevolence? With Sensei, his benevolent nature seemed to originate from his sense of fair-mindedness. It wasn't about being kind to me; rather, it was born from a teacherly attitude of being willing to listen to my opinion without prejudice. I found this considerably more wonderful than just being nice to me.

That was quite a discovery for me, the fact that arbitrary kindness makes me uncomfortable, but that being treated fairly feels good.

"So there's nothing to worry about if something happens," I reasoned.

To which Sensei widened his eyes and asked, "Something like what?"

"Anything."

"So then, what?"

"Um, for instance, you could be carrying something with both hands full when suddenly it starts raining, and there aren't any public phones nearby, and now it's crowded with people under the shop awnings, and you have to get home quickly—something like that."

"Tsukiko, in that situation I would just get wet going home."

"But what if the thing you're carrying couldn't get wet? Like some kind of bomb that would ignite if it got wet."

"I would never buy anything like that."

"What if there were a dangerous character lurking in the shadows?"

"It's just as likely that there would be a dangerous character lurking somewhere when I'm walking down the street with you, Tsukiko."

"What if you slipped on the wet sidewalk on your way?"

"Tsukiko, you're the one who falls, aren't you? I train in the mountains."

Everything Sensei said was right. I fell silent and cast my eyes downward.

"Tsukiko," Sensei said softly after a moment. "I understand. I will get a mobile phone."

What? I asked.

Sensei patted the top of my head and replied, "You never know when something might happen to us geezers."

"You're not a geezer, Sensei!" I contradicted him.

"In return . . ."

"What?"

In return, Tsukiko, I ask you not to call it a cell. Please refer to it as a mobile phone. I insist. I can't stand to hear people call it a cell.

And that's how Sensei came to have a mobile phone. Every so often I call it, just for practice. Sensei has only ever called me from it once.

"Sensei?"

"Yes?"

"Um, I'm at Satoru's place."

"Yes."

"Yes" is all Sensei ever says. This might not be so unusual, but on a mobile phone, it becomes remarkable.

"Will you join me?"

"Yes."

"I'm so pleased."

"Likewise."

At last, an utterance other than "Yes." Satoru grinned. He came out from behind the counter and went to hang the curtain outside, still grinning. I scooped some more miso paste with my finger and licked it. The aroma of *oden* cooking filled the bar.

THERE WAS ONE thing I was concerned about.

Sensei and I had not yet slept together.

I was concerned about it in the same way that I might be about the looming shadow of menopause that I already felt or about worrisome gamma-GTP levels in my liver function when I went for a checkup. When it comes to the workings of the human body, the brain, the internal organs, and the genitals were all part of the same whole. I became aware of this because of Sensei's age.

I may have been concerned, but that's not to say that I was frustrated by it. And if we never slept together, well, that was how it would be. But as for Sensei himself, he seemed to have quite a different attitude.

"Tsukiko, I'm a bit anxious," Sensei said to me one day.

We were at Sensei's house, eating *yudofu*. Since it was the middle of the day, Sensei had prepared *yudofu* in an alumite pot for us to eat while we drank some beer. He made it with cod and chrysanthemum greens. When I made *yudofu*, tofu was the only ingredient. As I sat there, my head a little fuzzy from drinking in the daytime, it had occurred to me that this was how people who didn't know each other developed a familiarity.

"Anxious?"

"Er, well, it's been a long time since I was with my wife."

Oh, I exclaimed, my mouth half-open. I was careful not to let Sensei stick in his finger, though. Ever since that time, Sensei would quickly poke his finger into my half-open mouth if I let my guard down. He was much more playful than I had realized.

"It's fine, if we don't do that," I said hurriedly.

"By 'that,' do you mean what I think you mean?" Sensei's expression was serious.

"Not 'that,' per se," I replied as I readjusted myself, sitting on my heels.

Sensei nodded gravely. "Tsukiko, physical intimacy is essential. No matter how old you are, it's extremely important." He had assumed a firm tone, like back in the day when he would read aloud from *The Tale of the Heike* at his teacher's podium.

"However, I don't have any confidence that I'm capable of it. If I were to try when I was feeling insecure, and then if I couldn't do it, my confidence would be even more diminished. And that is such a formidable outcome that it prevents me from even trying." *The Tale of the Heike* continued.

"I sincerely apologize." Sensei bowed deeply, concluding *The Tale of the Heike*. Still seated on my heels, I bowed too.

Uh, why don't I help you? I wanted to say. We could give it a try soon. But, feeling the pressure of Sensei's solemnity, I didn't feel like I could say this to him. Nor could I tell him I didn't give a damn about that. Or that I would rather he just go on kissing and holding me like always.

Since I couldn't say any of these things, I poured some beer into Sensei's glass. Sensei opened wide and drank it down, and I ladled some cod out of the pot. Chrysanthemum greens clung to the fish, creating a lovely contrast of green and white. Isn't that pretty, Sensei? I said, and Sensei smiled. Then he patted the top of my head, as always, over and over.

WE WENT TO all kinds of places on our dates. Sensei preferred to call them "dates," using the English word.

"Let's go on a date," Sensei would say. Even though we lived close to each other, we always met up at the station nearest the location of our date. We would make our separate ways to the station. If we ever ran into each other on the train on the way to meet up, Sensei would murmur something like, Oh-ho, Tsukiko, what a strange place to see you.

The place we went most often was the aquarium. Sensei loved to see the fish.

"When I was a little boy, I used to love to look at illustrated guides to fish," Sensei explained.

"How old were you then?"

"I must have been in elementary school."

Sensei had shown me a picture from when he was an elementary student. In the faded, sepia-toned photograph, Sensei was wearing a sailor hat and squinting his eyes as if it were too bright.

"You were cute," I said.

Sensei nodded and said, "Well, Tsukiko, you're *still* cute."

Sensei and I stood in front of the migratory fish tank that held tuna and skipjack. Watching the fish go round and round in one direction, I was struck by the feeling that we had been standing there like this for a very long time, the two of us.

"Sensei?" I ventured.

"What is it, Tsukiko?"

"I love you, Sensei."

"I love you too, Tsukiko."

We spoke these words to each other sincerely. We were always sincere with each other. Even when we were joking around, we were sincere. Come to think of it, so were the tuna. And the skipjack. All living things were sincere, on the whole.

We also went to Disneyland, of course. As we were watching the evening parade, Sensei shed a few tears. I did too. Each of us, though together, was probably thinking of different things that made us cry.

"There is something wistful about the lights at night," Sensei said as he blew his nose on a big white handkerchief.

"Sensei, you cry sometimes, don't you?"

"With few exceptions, geezers are easily moved to tears."

"I love you, Sensei."

Sensei didn't reply. He was watching the parade intently. His profile illuminated, Sensei's eyes appeared sunken. Sensei, I said, but he didn't reply at all. Once again I called Sensei, and there was no reply. I held on tightly to Sensei's arm with my own and gazed out at Mickey and the little people and Sleeping Beauty.

"I had fun on our date," I said.

"I did too." At last he replied to me.

"I hope you'll ask me out again."

"I will."

"Sensei?"

"Yes?"

"Sensei?"

"Yes?"

"Please don't go away."

"I'm not going anywhere."

The parade music grew significantly louder, and the little people leapt around. The procession finally began to recede. Sensei and I were left in the darkness. Bringing up the end of the line was Mickey, swinging his hips as he slowly walked along. Sensei and I held hands in the darkness. Then I shivered the slightest bit.

SHOULD I TELL the story of the only time that Sensei ever called me from his mobile phone?

I could hear background noise, which was how I knew he was using the mobile phone.

"Tsukiko?" Sensei said.

"Yes?"

"Tsukiko?"

"Yes?"

In a reversal of our usual roles, I became the one who said only "Yes."

"Tsukiko, you really are such a lovely girl."

"What?"

That was all he said before abruptly hanging up. I called him right back, but he didn't answer. About two hours later I called Sensei at home, and this time he answered, his voice perfectly serene.

"What was that, before?"

"Nothing, I just suddenly thought of it."

"Where were you calling from?"

"By the greengrocery near the station."

The greengrocery? I echoed.

I bought *daikon* and spinach at the greengrocery, Sensei replied.

I laughed, and Sensei laughed too on the other end of the line.

"Tsukiko, come quickly," Sensei said suddenly.

"To your house?"

"Yes."

I grabbed a toothbrush and pajamas and face lotion, throwing them into a bag and scurrying over to Sensei's house. Sensei stood at the gate to meet me. He took my hand as we went inside to the tatami room where Sensei laid out the futon. I put sheets on the futon. It was like an assembly line as we made the bed.

Without saying a word, Sensei and I collapsed on top of the futon. It was the first time Sensei had embraced me passionately and deeply.

I spent that night at Sensei's house, sleeping beside him. In the morning when he opened the rain shutters, the berries on the laurel trees gleamed lustrously in the morning sun. Bulbuls came to peck at the berries. Their warbling song echoed throughout Sensei's garden. Shoulder to shoulder, Sensei and I gazed out at them.

Tsukiko, you're such a lovely girl, Sensei said.

Sensei, I love you, I replied. The bulbuls warbled their song.

IT ALL SEEMS like so long ago. The time that I spent with Sensei—at first faint, then deepening in intensity—passed me by. Two years from when we encountered each other for the second time. Three years once we began what Sensei referred to as our "official relationship." That was all the time we shared together.

And since that time, there's precious little that could be done about it.

I have Sensei's briefcase. Sensei left it to me.

His son didn't much resemble Sensei. He had stood silently before me, bowing, and at that moment something about his stance reminded me vaguely of Sensei.

"You were very kind to my dad, Harutsuna, before he died," his son said, bowing deeply.

When I heard him speak Sensei's name, Harutsuna, my tears welled up. And I had hardly cried up until that point. I was able to cry when I thought about him as Harutsuna Matsumoto, like a stranger. I was able to cry when I realized that Sensei had already gone away somewhere, before I ever came to know him well.

Sensei's briefcase lies beside my dressing table. Once in a while I still go to Satoru's place. Not as often as before. Satoru doesn't say anything. He's always moving about, busy at work. It's warm inside the bar, and there have been times when I even doze off. One mustn't behave so poorly in public, I'm sure Sensei would say.

> In loneliness I have drifted this long way, alone.
> My torn and shabby robe could not keep out the cold.
> And tonight the sky was so clear
> it made my heart ache all the more.

Sensei taught me this poem by Seihaku Irako at some point. I try reading it and other poems out loud when I'm home alone. I've been studying a bit since you passed away, Sensei, I murmur.

Sometimes when I call out, Sensei, I can hear a voice reply from the ceiling above, Tsukiko. I've started making *yudofu* like you, Sensei, with cod and chrysanthemum greens. Sensei, I hope we see each other again one day, I say. And from the ceiling, Sensei replies, Surely we shall see each other one day.

Those nights, I open Sensei's briefcase and peer inside. The blank empty space unfolds, containing nothing within. It holds nothing more than an expanse of desolate absence.